S0-ARW-968

# THE
# WIND CHIME
# TALES

### By Larry Incollingo
#### Copyright 1997
#### All Rights Reserved

## Published By Reunion Books
### 3949 Old SR 446
### Bloomington, IN 47401

### Cover Design
### R.L. Robertson

## Other Books By Larry Incollingo
*Laughing All The Way*
*G'bye My Honey*
*Precious Rascal*
*Ol' Sam Payton*
*ECHOES of Journeys Past*
*The Tin Can Man*

### SEND A GIFT COPY TO A FRIEND
*See coupon in back of book to order*

# ACKNOWLEDGMENT

I shall always be grateful to my lovely wife Marion for keeping a happy and cozy home, and the household checkbook balanced, while I am engrossed in my work. - LInc.

Who has seen the wind?
Neither you nor I:
But when the wind chimes sing their song,
The wind is passing by.*

# CONTENTS

# THE WIND CHIME

After she was felled by illness, Ruth Harger's heart was in a seriously weakened condition. She was ordered to refrain from sweeping and dusting, making beds, cooking and doing all those things a homemaker does.

"Bed," the doctor ordered. "Go to bed and stay there," he told her. "Or," he added, "you will not be long for this world."

One Wednesday, when the sun was shining brightly and the windchill was doing unkind things with the mid-March temperature in Owensburg, Ruth was participating in an annual spring ritual. She was raking leaves left over from the past fall, picking up sticks that had dropped from a tree, and crawling around on her hands and knees cleaning flower beds.

When she was finished with those chores she adjusted her head scarf against a brisk wind and walked to the post office to pick up the day's mail. On the return walk she stopped off at the general store. I was there, and we greeted each other with a hug and a buss on the cheek, during which I said, "I love you Ruth," and sat down at a table with her for a visit.

Ruth was given that awful fatalistic ultimatum some three or four decades before that Wednesday.

She couldn't remember exactly when, or she didn't care to. Either way was all right with me. She was old enough to do as she pleased. Midway between eighty and ninety, at this time, she had a simple explanation for not being in a grave.

"As the missionary told the cannibal," she quipped with a smile, "you can't keep a good man down."

After hearing the sentence given her so long ago, Ruth had taken a job at Western Michigan University, in Kalamazoo, and worked enough years there to assure herself of a pension. Having fallen in love with the tranquility and the people of the small Hoosier community of Owensburg during a visit many years ago, she took up residence there after her retirement.

"Mom used to say that you can do a lot of things if you take Willie along," she said of outliving her doctor's prediction, her doctor, and making it to the brink of the 21st Century.

"You don't know Willie – Will Power?" she feigned amazement in my direction. "Oh, I think he's wonderful." Then extending her thumb ceilingward she added, "I thank Him every day, too. When I get out of bed in the morning it's the first thing I do. I thank God. Then I say, 'Now let's get goin' again, God.' And I take Him along with me in everything that I do."

She couldn't remember when she last took medicine for something, or aspirin for anything.

"I don't even have headaches," she said. "I read everything I can get my hands on, watch television, write my own checks, and keep my own balance so that I never bounce one. I can do for myself."

A native of Rosedale, Indiana, she spent the early years in Lyford, a small community between Clinton and Terre Haute. She went to Kalamazoo as a young woman.

2

"I wasn't yet seventeen when I got married, and before I was twenty-two I had four little children dragging around after me," she slowly shook her head at the memory. "I had a good marriage, but after he died I didn't want another husband." She laughed. "If you burn your fingers you don't go back to the fire," she said.

Anyone watching might have wondered about us when Ruth and I hugged the way we did, and after hearing what I said. We had been friends ever since we visited in her kitchen one winter day a long time before that. It was a visit I cherish. We talked while comfortably seated at the kitchen table. I couldn't help but notice then that every time the furnace blower kicked on the flow of forced air above us moved the delicate cymbals of a cluster of wind chimes hanging from the kitchen ceiling.

It was a tiny, fragile sound – a subtle *ting, ting* – that was simultaneously tenderly sweet and soothing. In a calming way it kept diverting my attention. I remember being moved to wonder why everyone didn't have wind chimes like hers in their kitchen. But there was another reason the soft sounds of the wind chimes stuck with me.

During our visit Ruth had mentioned Merla Craig, who then served as the pastor of the Owensburg Baptist Church. She was telling me how pleased she was that the peace she'd found in Owensburg was enhanced by having Mr. Craig as her minister, when I recalled that he was the same man who had spoken at the funeral of a friend some time earlier.

She was Velma (Dutch) Lockhart, probably one of the best euchre players I had ever known, and surely one of the cleverest who had ever turned a bower. I remembered having agreed with Ruth, after she had brought up the subject, that it was indeed a difficult thing to do, to go to the funeral home when a good friend is lying there dead. Ruth spoke of having done that.

Dutch was such a friend. She was a young friend, too. And there, in Ruth's kitchen, with the wind chimes *ting-tinging,* the memory flashed through my mind. I remembered that when I had entered the mortuary in Bedford at the time of Dutch's viewing, I was met by my youngest daughter, Lisa, and it was obvious that she'd been weeping. But tears were flowing all around us, for Dutch had many friends.

A stout, balding man had stood up and begun the eulogy, and soon the silence resonated to the sound of his words, gentle and kind. He spoke of Dutch and God and life, and he spoke of the living of life and the death of it. His manner and speech touched each of us deeply, saddening us while at the same time refreshing us. My daughter's tears dried up, and the tears around us ceased.

This was a special man; this was Merla Craig. I remembered the first time I'd been in his company. Somewhat portly, dressed in bib overalls and green-billed cap, for he was a farmer, too, he was at the peak of the fulfillment of a dream.

"From the time I was a boy growing up in Silverville I had a longing to be the pastor of a small church and to be a small farmer," he had told me as we stood in the driveway of his home  on the Fayetteville-Coxton Road. "And I suppose you'd say that is what I am."

The dream had begun taking shape for him in 1943 when he was asked to speak before a bi-weekly service at the Owensburg Baptist Church. Most of the young men of that time were going off to war and he hoped to join them.

4

"So, figuring I'd be drafted in a little while, anyway, I accepted what I thought would be a temporary thing," he said.

But war for him was not meant to be and he continued preaching and farming. "I dreamed of building Owensburg Baptist large enough to have a full-time pastor," he recalled. "I was working every day and would hold service every two weeks for nine people. The collection would come to seven dollars, and five of that was my tithe."

But he didn't give up. And his determination had paid off handsomely. The Sunday before we spoke a hundred and twenty-two souls had attended the weekly Sunday morning worship at the church; a hundred and fifty more were counted at Sunday School.

"The Lord's been good to me," he told me. "I can't praise Him enough. And I'm very grateful."

Leading a church was never easy. It was never certain. On two separate occasions when attendance had fallen and interest seemed to wane, and the future of the church seemed to hang in the balance, Mr. Craig tried to persuade church members to bring in a new face, a new leader. Both times the faithful called at his home armed with facts and figures that left no doubt that Mr. Craig was wrong, that he was still the right man to lead them.

"I stayed," he said. "And I'm happy that I did. I don't know of any other place I'd rather be than at Owensburg Baptist Church come Sunday. That's the happiest place of my life, next to my home."

Home was a red brick dwelling he shared with Wanda Jewel Craig who was his girl when they were growing up in Silverville. They reared three daughters and one son there. As youngsters Merla and Wanda attended the old two-room Silverville School,

**Merla (Merlie) Craig**
A Day on the Farm

and on Sundays they listened to Ora Bolton preach at the Baptist Church there. It was Ora Bolton who detected the boy's shaping dream and later influenced his acceptance of the Owensburg pulpit. In the more than forty years that had passed, Merla had traveled untold numbers of miles between his home and the church, and between his home and so many other places, to officiate at weddings and funerals.

"I've always given funerals priority over everything else in my life," he revealed to me that day. "I have never kept count of how many I've preached, but we have estimated a thousand two-hundred and fifty, up to this time."

Among the deceased were believers from all walks of life, in rural areas and in cities and in towns for miles around.

"Many of them I never knew," he confessed. "Some had heard me preach the funeral of a friend or a loved one and just let it be known that, 'When I die I want Merlie (he is known to almost everyone as Merlie) to preach my funeral.' I was always glad to go. Sometimes people couldn't afford to give me anything, and one time someone gave me two dollars. But I never let that stand in the way of preaching a person's funeral. I was just as glad to go for nothing. I'm the kind of person who has never had trouble loving people. I just take them for what they are and go from there to a better life with them. I don't know anyone I don't love."

This, then, was the soft-spoken, loving man who preached Dutch's funeral. As I listened to him I was, at least for the moment, anxious to believe that there was a purpose to death, that there was meaning to the annihilation of life, that something better, something more glorious than life on this earth, lay beyond the grave. And in that fleeting moment I was, or so I thought, able to understand why Dutch had to leave so soon.

As I continued to listen there in the funeral home, another memory entered the colorfully active stage of my mind. It had been only a few days earlier, a Monday afternoon, that I had answered my telephone in the newsroom and heard Dutch's voice, gay and lighthearted.

"In two days I'll be going home," the words seemed bursting with assurance as they came over the phone. "And with plenty of rest, my doctor thinks he'll get me well. I won't be able to work again," there was a slight downward pitch to the tone of her voice, "but I'll have a life."

It was precisely for the same reason that ten years earlier she had undergone open heart surgery at Dunn Memorial Hospital in Bedford. I remembered having marveled at her courage after her surgery. Slightly over five feet tall and about ninety pounds, she was tiny, and, I thought, almost helpless. But she was alive, and jubilant. It was not only her first open heart surgery, it was the first surgery of its kind performed at that hospital, and in larger cities for miles around. And Dutch was effusively happy over its outcome.

Open heart surgery even in the great medical centers of that period was a scary, uncertain prospect. National magazines and newswire services almost weekly carried accounts of "miracle" open heart surgeries performed by renowned surgeons in large hospitals in major cities around the U.S. In a small hospital in a small town in rural Indiana such an operation was unheard of, and it must have been a frightful one to undergo. But when her physician had convinced her that all would be well, and she heard similar assur-

8

**Velma Walls Lockhart**
(Dutch)
The Early Days

ances from her surgeon, fear left her, she told me.

"I was never worried," she informed me at the time. "I knew I would come out of it all right. I knew I'd make it. And here I am. It was one of those 'do or don't' operations," she had bubbled. "You do it, or you don't live."

She exuded warm praise for her physician, the late Howard T. Hammel. And she praised a man to whom she referred only as "Dr. Shah," the surgeon who had repaired her heart and extended her life. He was Frank Shahbahrami, M.D., who subsequently moved his practice from Bedford twenty-five miles away to Bloomington and Bloomington Hospital.

A country girl, Dutch, at a young age, had married legendary southern Indiana gambler and Marengo native Jack Lockhart, who operated one of Bedford's more popular honky-tonks. This was the beginning of a twenty-four year stint in that tavern. When Jack died fifteen years after their marriage she operated the place on her own. At the same time she had managed to devote her life to her children.

During the years of her marriage to Lockhart she had learned to mix drinks, deal five-card stud, and to listen. As a mixer of drinks and as a listener she fit the needs of the new owners of the tavern each time it was sold and was employed by them. As a poker and, especially, euchre player she sat in such games where she happened to find them. In this role she had acquired a host of friends.

They were not high society people, yet they were not unsavory, nor were they criminals. They simply were not the kind of friends the average lady might accumulate in a lifetime. But they had a single trait in common; they had a rough-hewn affection for Dutch. They were among the number who appeared at her bedside after her first surgery. They were around in the years that followed to imbibe at the bar from which she dispensed drinks. They played poker and euchre with and against her. The products of a variety of backgrounds, they had come from good homes, mediocre homes, bad homes, rich homes, not so rich homes, even foster homes. But they came to see Dutch.

When they learned of her impending second open-heart surgery on April 24, 1979, at the Indiana University Medical Center in Indianapolis, they offered her the greatest gifts they possessed – their hopes and prayers. Some even went to churches to light votive candles .

"They've all been so good to me," she expressed her gratitude to me one day before that second surgery. "And with friends like that," she laughed, "how can I lose?"

She was thoughtful for a moment. Then she said with a rush of feeling, "Deep inside I know I'm going to make it. Deep inside I know that I'm going to get well."

In the months following that second surgery she began to weaken, to experience a shortness of breath. She eventually was admitted to Bloomington Hospital. On that December afternoon that we spoke on the phone, Dutch was reclining in bed there.

"There's no way," she had said of a desire and the desperate need to return to work to pay her living expenses, "I couldn't cut it."

Although she seemed happy, her optimism of past years and months was gone. There was no doubt that Dutch was a sick woman, and that she also was aware of her condition. But Christmas was only days away and like the rest of us, Dutch was eagerly looking forward to the holiday. She spoke of going home. She was excited about being with her children, her grandchildren, her widowed father, Alpha Walls, whom she dearly loved and who was then eighty-two years old, and her siblings. Never before, she told me that afternoon on the phone, had she looked so eagerly to a Christmas. "I'll be going home Wednesday," she said. "The doctor told me today that I should be well enough by then. I'm so happy."

"I'm going to try to see you tomorrow," I promised when she invited me to visit her at the hospital. "But if I don't see you at the hospital I'll see you at home."

Being the season of Christmas it was a busy time. By noon Tuesday I knew that I could not squeeze a hospital visit before Wednesday. I dialed the hospital to explain to Dutch, and to wish her a pleasant trip home, a successful convalescence, and a Merry Christmas.

"Are you a relative?" I was asked by a hospital official who came on the phone.

"No," I replied. "I'm just a friend." I gave my name. "She's scheduled to go home tomorrow," I said. "I can't get over there before then, so I want to say goodbye now, and Merry Christmas."

"I'm sorry," the woman's voice was apologetic. "Mrs. Lockhart died at eleven o'clock this morning."

Other memories of Dutch filled my mind. It was of some comfort to remember an incident from her April stay at the IU Med Center. I had written a column about her second open heart surgery.

"I got cards and letters from everywhere," she later bubbled to me. "I got so many they'd deliver them each day with a rubber band around them. It was just wonderful."

The pain of not having visited Dutch in Bloomington Hospital stayed with me a long time. I still regret not having done so. I remember that I made a promise to myself that it would not happen again. Yet it has. I have waited too long to visit sick friends, too long to write, too long to telephone. I regret having done so, yet I continue to make the same mistake. My intentions are above reproach, but my actions fall far short of that. Still, I have learned a lesson. When I greet or part company with friends like Ruth Harger, I am not ashamed to embrace them and say, "I love you." For it may be the last time we see each other.

Because of Ruth's determination to live, there is a kind of unutterable bond between her and me, as there is between Mr. Craig and Dutch and me, and so many others, as you will find as you continue reading this book. Hopefully you too share a similar bond with people, and there is a sound, like the gentle *ting-ting* of wind chimes, that brings pleasant recollections of them.

# ALBERT

The Bloomington Hospital emergency room nurse took one look at the man's back and gasped, "Goodness! What in the world happened to you?"

Albert Skirvin was bleeding from a large crooked-cross cut on his back, and from a severed artery in his right arm.

The gaping red wound extended from just below his right ear, across his back to his left waist, and then from one side of his back to the other, ending at the artery in his right arm.

"Well," said Albert, "They say you're supposed to bring in your man, or look like you at least tried. Wouldn't you say I look like I tried?"

The year was 1939. Albert Skirvin was a young Monroe County deputy sheriff during the term of Sheriff Earl Baxter. He was enjoying a vacation at home with his wife Eva when a neighbor knocked on the door and asked him to please intervene in a family dispute. In the living room of that same home, on East Third Street, in Bloomington, one day, Albert showed me photographs taken of his back after that fracas.

"I had my man," Albert said, explaining that he had merely teased the nurse at the hospital. "When I left

14

my house that day I picked up a pair of handcuffs, and after he cut me I got them on him." When the emergency room physician suggested putting him to sleep for the stitching process, Albert said he replied, "I wasn't sleeping when I got it. Go ahead and sew."

And to me he explained that decision with these words: "A fellow's got to stay awake and on the move or die."

This same determination was to reveal itself publicly again in the early to mid-Forties when Albert served two two-year terms as sheriff, as was the custom then. Within days after its occurrence, Albert, as Sheriff Albert Skirvin, solved the 1946 double-murder at Hunter Valley Mill.

In that same year, a decapitated corpse, dead for two weeks, was found in a pine grove southeast of Bloomington. Thirty days after that grim discovery, Albert was on his way to the prison at Michigan City with the killer who had been sentenced to life.

"All you needed then was nerve enough to tie into them," Albert said of dealing with murderers and other criminals. "Now you get all tangled up with lawyers and laws."

But it was more than just nerve that made him a good and likable and respected policeman. He put it in these words.

"If I thought a man was guilty I worked hard to get the evidence against him. If I didn't think a man was guilty, I worked hard to prove he was innocent. I was always honest, and I never lied to get a man convicted."

Policing – sheriffing, it was called until recent years – got into Albert's blood, and during six subsequent campaigns the voters of Monroe County were to see

15

the name Albert Skirvin on the ballot. He ran some close races, but he was defeated each time.

"I never did want him to run," Eva remembered his political successes and disappointments. "Living down there (in the jail) is no family life. I wouldn't recommend it to anyone."

Albert and Eva were married in a double ceremony with Don Foster and Edna McCoy in 1935. The Skirvins had two sons, Donald and Ted, and seven grandchildren.

Eva spent thirty-one years in the same office, in the photographic laboratory in the Audio Visual Center at Indiana University in Bloomington before her retirement. She then devoted her time to Albert and oil painting. The walls of the Skirvin home served as exhibit panels for her works.

During Sheriff Clifford Thrasher's first four-year term, one of his most popular deputies was Albert Skirvin. Younger lawmen enjoyed listening to the older man relate his experiences as sheriff, when he and two deputies were the only law in the county. They called him Albert, or Al, or Skirv, and they tried to envision and emulate him as he was in his younger days.

"We had no uniforms back then," Albert used to tell them. "We dressed like anyone else."

One of his memories was of a particularly incorrigible prisoner he was preparing to deliver by auto to Pendleton. He had two deputies at this time and one of them offered to accompany him, in the event the prisoner might try to escape and do bodily harm to Albert in the process.

Albert refused, saying, "No, I'll take him by myself. That way if anything happens there will be only one story to tell."

He was to later get a pleasant surprise from that

**Albert Skirvin**
Sheriffing

delinquent. But I'll save telling that until the end of this story about Albert.

When he wasn't sheriffing, or running for that office, Albert sold real estate.

"I graduated from the 'Harry Stephens Real Estate School,'" he joked, dating himself to a 1947 beginning in that field.

"You didn't have to have a license then, and most of us old-timers started with Harry Stephens," Albert explained, "and we always said we graduated from the Harry Stephens Real Estate School."

For twenty years he drove a school bus, hauling over the years hundreds of school children to Unionville. His last political campaign was in the Monroe County sheriff's primary in 1974. A popular, handsome, smiling man of sixty-four, Albert's love for police work received a telling blow. He was defeated again.

On the 31st day of December, that year, Monroe County schools were in vacation. Albert, that morning, got out of bed, rose to his feet, and collapsed with a stroke. In the hospital he held my hand but could not grip it. Weeks later, in the Bloomington Convalescent Center, he did grip my hand.

Sixty-four days from the day he was taken from his home by ambulance, Albert Skirvin again revealed the determination that would not let him sleep in the hospital emergency room that night in 1939; he walked unaided across the threshold of his home.

That was March 6, 1975, and when I visited Albert one morning after that, he called from the bedroom, saying, "Larry, I've got a surprise for you."

He appeared in the bedroom doorway and held aloft a cane, and he walked, unaided and unsupported, to a couch and sat down.

"Determination had a lot to do with it," he admitted

proudly, 'But," and to make what he believed was an important point his mood seemed to change dramatically, "there was a lot of praying, too, by a lot of people."

Many of those people who prayed had stopped at the Skirvin home to visit with him. One visitor to Albert's home was Monroe County Sheriff Bill (Brownie) Brown.

"August 20th was my birthday," Albert said, his face brightening. "Brownie brought me this," and he handed me an official special deputy's card.

"You're still a cop, Albert," I said and Albert smiled his pleasure.

Then he told me about the cane he was carrying when he emerged from the bedroom.

"That fellow who gave me so much trouble that I took to Pendleton by myself? Well," he smiled, "he made it for me while he was up there. It's made from two kinds of wood."

# GIVE ME ANGEL AVENUE

Veva Cope relaxed in her chair. She raised her foot to the couch and rested it there. She couldn't have been more at ease – or so it seemed. She was recalling memories of her days as a telephone operator in the earlier days of Nashville in Brown County.

"We rarely said, 'Number please,' as they did in bigger towns of that time, or in the cities, before they were cut over to dial phones," Veva remembered. "There were these tabs that fell on the switchboard when someone took a receiver off a hook. We knew from the sound of a falling tab whose line it was."

When she first went to work for the independent Union Telephone Company, there were about fifty telephones in Nashville. Other independents were Oscar Frazer's phone company in New Bellesville, and another telephone company owned by Bill Exner, which was situated at Belmont.

"I knew a lot of voices in those days," Veva continued her recollections. "When I'd recognize the sound of a tab falling, I knew who to expect on the line. After I heard the voice I knew for sure who it was.

"So when a tab would fall I'd plug in and just say 'Yes?' or, 'What can I do for you,' or something like that.

"I remember," she laughed, "there was this one man who would say, 'Give me Angel Avenue,' and I knew he meant his home. So I'd ring his wife. Another man would get on the line and say, 'Ring Jenny for me,' and I knew that Jenny was his wife. And I'd ring his home.

"There were others who would call for their relatives or friends and I knew what line to plug into just by the name. One of those," she smiled, "was a woman named Sister Sarah. People would call in and say, 'Give me Sister Sarah,' and I'd ring her line."

In those days a woman named Catherine Norris was a midwife who was much sought after in Nashville because the village then was without a doctor.

"I used to know pretty well how to find her, wherever she was," Veva remembered. "She was wanted so much, I had to know."

When she was able to locate the midwife and dispatch her in time to the home of an anxious male caller one day, Veva was in for a surprise. Most appreciatively the man named his new-born daughter Veva, after the telephone operator who'd spared him what he believed would have been an ordeal.

Indiana Bell bought the independent company in 1954, and two years later Nashville was cut to dial phones. Veva, then an employee of the new owner, was needed in Morgantown. Later she was sent to a little town, near Elwood, named Aroma. She worked in Fishers, near Indianapolis, then Oaklandon. But the memories, during our visit in the apartment where she lived alone, were of Nashville, and Veva recalled a couple more.

"A pool room across the street from the telephone office burned one night," she said. "Our home, mine and my two sons' home, was in the telephone office. That was part of my salary as agent – chief operator.

21

That fire was so hot a lineman had to pour water on the cable to keep it from burning. It was so hot it cracked the windows on buildings across the street.

"I had to call out all the firemen," she continued. "And while it was burning I had to call all the property owners of other businesses."

While townspeople warned her that she should get out, Veva remained at the switchboard. Furthermore, she encouraged other women to make hot coffee in the kitchen of the living quarters and to carry it to the firemen. Several buildings were destroyed in the blaze.

"Being a telephone operator," she began the second memory, "you always knew when tragedy or disaster struck. And if it was a drowning, or some other terrible thing where kids might be involved, if my two sons weren't right where I could see them, I would just about climb a tree until I found out where they were."

When the late Governor George Craig entered the telephone office one night to use its facilities, he looked at Veva and said, "Excuse me. I know it's not you girls (there were additional operators working there by this time), but something smells in here."

It cost Indiana Bell five-hundred dollars to find the source; a raccoon that had earlier crawled into a small space between a wall and the floor and died there.

Veva was born at Needmore, in Brown County, where her father, Fletcher Poling, the first Illinois-Central Railroad agent at Trevlac, settled with his bride Margaret Barrick. The IC had just been built through Brown County on the Indianapolis, Ind. to Effingham, Ill. run. When he later was appointed post master at Nashville the family, Veva, and two sisters, Marie and Mable, moved to the village. Veva was then nine.

"This is home," Veva said of her life in the small

town. "I wouldn't trade Nashville for all the tea in China. There is no place near as good as Nashville."

While never an aspirant to political office, Veva did serve as county treasurer and clerk. After the resignation of Janet McFarland in 1971, Veva was appointed to that office and served there until the end of 1982. Following the untimely death of newly reelected clerk Millard (Mid) Thickston, and the subsequent resignation of Paul Rogers who was appointed to serve out his term, Veva was tagged to fill that office. She was also Republican ("All of us Polings were Republicans") county chairman at the time.

Veva had moved her chair several times during our visit, and she had adjusted and readjusted her leg on the couch as she talked.

Because of a diabetic condition, a foot infection had led to the amputation the previous April of Veva's right leg above the knee. The chair from which she spoke during our visit was a wheelchair, to which she had been confined since her recuperation in three hospitals and one extended care center.

"Those are memories I don't care to recall," she said. "Especially that extended care center. When I get to feeling sorry for myself I think of that place and I'm all better, just like that. I don't ever – never again – want to go into a place like that."

Life also brightened when she moved from a home near Jackson Branch to an apartment on Artist Drive, in Nashville, where I visited with her.

"I can get out here," she compared the easy accessibility from the apartment to the out of doors to the many steps of her former residence. "And friends find it easier to take me out from here, too."

With the out of doors in mind, Veva looked forward to spring.

"I can even get out myself, then," she said. "I won't be of any trouble to anyone."

There was another reason for her forward look. Veva expected to be fitted in April for a prosthesis. And she fully expected to be walking – without assistance – shortly after that.

And after that? The mother of two sons, grandmother to seven, and great grandmother to one, further revealed her courage.

"I'd like to have a job," she said. "An office job. Preferably one in Nashville. Then," her bright blue eyes twinkled over a smile, "there are lots of places I want to go."

# ENOCH'S BOYS

On the occasion of his father's death in 1915, T. Perry Wesley, in the first line of his autobiography, quoted an anonymous Kentuckian as saying, "I don't know what will become of Enoch's boys."

The man who spoke those words was among several people in the barnlot of the Enoch Wesley home in Yosemite (yo-se-mite), Kentucky. The event was the sale of the last of Enoch's worldly possessions – an old cow.

At the time of his death Enoch's boys numbered four: Irwin, Lofton, Mark, and T. Perry who then was ten years old.

In his book, "Datelines and By-Lines," which is subtitled "From Yosemite to Spencer," T. Perry revealed some of what became of them. Following military service in World War I, brothers Irwin and Lofton shook off the dust of Kentucky hill country and obtained jobs in Indianapolis. Brother Mark enrolled at Berea College, and T. Perry, along with their step-mother, Emma, eventually traveled north to Indianapolis to reassemble the family there.

"I had walked into a different world," T. Perry once said of the change from 1919 rural Kentucky to the Hoosier capital city. "There was very little of anything down in Yosemite, not over a half dozen automobiles in the whole county; it was backwoods."

On his twenty-second birthday, while he was still living in Indianapolis, something happened in Owen County that would later dramatically change his life: the *Evening World* daily newspaper was born in Spencer.

About twenty-one years later, in 1948, when T. Perry, by then a practiced and respected newspaperman, was looking for a newspaper to buy, a Spencer publisher named Carl Ward happened to have one for sale.

Because of the *World's* history since its founding on June 29, 1927, it was not unexpected that T. Perry would be thought of as just another in a succession of owners of the paper. But when he terminated its wire news service contract and opened its pages to only local news, dubious critics were forced to reappraise the paper's new owner.

"I was convinced that people in places like this wanted local news from their local newspaper," T. Perry said.

He wasn't wrong. The *World,* as a strictly local news daily was a big hit. And before long its circulation had doubled from 1,500 subscribers to 3,000, at a time when the total Owen County population was only 11,400.

"We became the people's newspaper," T. Perry observed. "We did away with a prescribed writing style. We put the news in the paper as it came to us from the people. And we had no deadlines. That hasn't changed. There was one deadline – classified advertisements had to be in by 9 a.m. of the day they were to run, and that continues to be the policy of the newspaper. But the paper has no set style and there are no other deadlines."

After the death of his wife, Aline, in 1959, T. Perry decided to sell the successful small town daily.

26

"I was in my forties when I came here," he said. "I was the owner, but when you own a small newspaper you are everything else, too. I was the typesetter, composer, mechanic, editor, layout man, janitor, reporter and circulation manager. My wife was the bookkeeper and ran the business office. When she died I'd had the paper about twelve years and had reached a point where I knew I wasn't capable of developing it the way I wanted, so I decided to sell," he said.

On the fifth of July, 1960, when new owner John T. Gillaspy took over, T. Perry became editor emeritus.

"Editor emeritus," he joked about his new status at the *World*, "means that they put you on a shelf, and twice a year they take you down, dust you off, then put you back on the shelf."

Not quite true. The experience and knowledge of a lifelong newsman and successful, award-winning publisher such as T. Perry are invaluable assets to any paper. The difference is that ensconced in a quiet office space he was able to devote his time to more enjoyable, if not more important, forms of writing and recording. In his words at the time, "I write what I want when I want," he said.

When he was in the notion he wrote another of his popular columns which appeared in the *World* under the wooden head "Now and Then." The name pertained more to the time of the column's appearance in the paper rather than to its content. But there were no strict rules, as the following doggerel about a still very busy newsman will attest.

27

**T. Perry Wesley**

# I AIN'T GOT TIME FOR HEAVEN, LORD
## By T. Perry Wesley

The good Lord said to me one day, I've got a place for you to stay.

You oughta stop, no more to roam, and come up here to make your home.

I said, well Lord, I'll wait a while, to get my lengthy reference file

In better shape than it's in now, I've got to get it done somehow.

And there's these columns yet to write, with many of them still in sight,

Such as one on Romona Road, and Canyon Inn's pie a la mode,

And one on Laymon's Twenty Grand, and lots of other stuff at hand.

There's just no end to what's to do, and I have finished such a few.

I need another month or so before I'd dare pick up and go.

But no, that wouldn't be enough for me to write up all that stuff,

Such as Viquesney's Doughboy thing, and one about the Brothers King.

And gosh! I almost clean forgot the one about the Cooper lot.

And then there's columns yet to do, about a dozen more or two.

And even that may not be all, for instance, some I don't recall,

Because there's many things to say about Sweet Owen day by day,

Such as the old log courthouse yarn, and one about the old log barn.

Of course there's one that has to be about that whopping big oak tree,
And I've just got to do one on that house of old Judge Robinson.
So, Lord, I think that you can see I'm stuck here through Eternity.
And when that's overwith and through, I'll still have lots of things to do.
So, as I think of things so far, don't keep those Pearly Gates ajar,
Cause, Lord, I think it's plain to see that I'll need all Eternity.
And when that's overwith and through, I'll still have things I've yet to do.


Queried about his greatest experience as a newspaperman, T. Perry replied, "I think the greatest – the best – was happening onto Spencer. When I think back, I have lived in three places in my life, but I have lived here three times longer than in any of those other places. I wasn't here six months until I became a native. This is where I wanted my roots."

On the 29th of June, 1997, T. Perry and the *World* would share birthday honors: he 92, the paper 70. No big deal. At the *World*, and in the world of newspapers, that date will be just another news day.

Except that when it arrives some of us may remember what became of one of Enoch's boys.

# THE SAGA OF SAM

A resident of the house next door, Sam was conspicuous for his long yellow hair and a disposition which, in a word, was cantankerous.

Sam was an aging boy cat.

Kitty Kat was a youthful calico girl cat with shapely legs and a swishing tail which at its very end curled coquettishly and seductively.

Kitty Kat lived at our house.

From the time she had come there as a kitten she and Sam had been glancing friends. From his front porch rail he would glance at her, and from the rail of our front porch where she frequently lounged Kitty Kat would glance at him. It seemed an innocent little game they played.

Being the prodigious nocturnal prowler that he was, Sam some days remained tiredly aloof from glancing and just lay there asleep. At other times he was sullenly busy licking newly acquired wounds suffered during his previous nighttime pursuits.

Kitty Kat was unchanging, gentle, loving, and from nose to tail she was the perfect leg-rubber. If she had a single characteristic which might have identified her with Sam it was the vicious whalebone stay in her body that occasionally came unsprung and landed her on an unsuspecting bird. Like Sam, Kitty Kat delighted in tearing them asunder and feasting on their tiny limbs.

Although they were much alike in that technique, Sam and Kitty Kat worked at it singly, never together. They were never together. They never wanted to be together. Well, never except once, and then chaos descended on our house.

The time they yearned to be together came during a summer's heat wave. We refused to allow Kitty Kat her usual freedom, and Sam began a protesting vigil and fast that was to continue for days. And before it was over we were sure they would kill him.

He took up an unyielding station on our front porch from where he'd call out to Kitty Kat in what sounded like the last moans of his life. "Nnnnowww!" he'd cry at brief intervals all through the day and especially at night. "MonOWTnowww! Nnnnowww!"

Confined as she was Kitty Kat was unable to respond to his mournful requests. But I went out. Several times. And each time I launched him off the porch with a broom. But each time he came right back and resumed his mournful serenade.

His suffering was too much for Kitty Kat, who we thought was too young to know better. Each time she heard him cry her eyes filled with pity and she'd curl the end of her tail and plead to go to his assistance. When we scolded her for her shameful behavior she'd sit back on her sleek haunches and call out to Sam, "MmwonletmeeOWtnowww!"

It went on for days. Nights. Kitty Kat would break it off every so often to eat and sleep and to rub against a leg or two. But Sam remained a study in perseverance and determination. And, as might have been expected, his continual serenading attracted the male population of Catville. With switchblades and brass knuckles they came to challenge what Sam believed was his private province.

Sam was no pushover. He placed his starved and parched body between them and our house where with pitched yowls and vicious snarls he held them off each night. When morning came the nocturnal visitors would retire to secret lairs for rest and rehabilitation. But not Sam. Without rest, food or drink, in temperatures that soared into the nineties, he patrolled the perimeter of our yard from front to back, across the back, back to front and across the front.

Stoically he marched through shimmering heat devils, often staggering from exhaustion, and stumbling over his tongue which hung out of his mouth almost to the ground. And each time a paw touched the broiling hot ground Sam would cry, "WOWWW! WOWWW! WOWWW!" And each time he made that awful sound his head would rise and fall. "WOWWW! WOWWW! WOWWW!"

One scorching hot afternoon during his long vigil Sam crawled to the shaded side of our front porch and lay there dying. Hanging out the side of his mouth his tongue jerked with every shallow breath he sucked into his laboring lungs. The long side of him puffed out and in like a power driven bellows. I felt a twinge of pity for him. But more than that I was aware of a deep respect for his moxie. Man to man, then, I placed a saucer of Kitty Kat's food and a cottage cheese container of water within easy reach on the porch floor. He was too far gone to touch them.

The lady next door, whom the kids called "Sam's mother," came over and tried coaxing and urging her pet to eat and drink. Sam appeared unable to raise his head, and we all agreed that he was finished. In one final effort to revive him, Sam's mother dumped the cottage cheese container of water over his head. He roused from his death throes in an explosion of new life that carried him over the porch rail and out on the broiling hot ground. There he resumed his patrol around the house, now crying as each high-stepping paw touched the hot pavement, "EE-OWWW! EE-OWWW! EE-OWWW!"

I can't remember if we got used to Sam's cries or if he simply gave up. But when we realized his song had in fact stopped we began looking around.

Sam was gone.

And so was Kitty Kat.

Just when we began thinking their disappearance was permanent they returned. Sam went to his house. Kitty Kat came to ours. Sam's mother kept him in intensive care for a few days until he regained his strength.

After that he was the same old cantankerous Sam, sitting on his front porch rail glancing now and then at Kitty Kat sitting on our front porch rail. Kitty Kat resumed her glancing from our porch rail too, but it no longer was an innocent little game between them. And she was never the same innocent Kitty Kat.

# RANGER RICK

When they learned she was pregnant with their first child, Richard (Rick) and Betty Jackson sold their automobile and used the money to buy a washing machine for Betty and a bicycle for Rick.

"I rode that bicycle to work and back home, and I used it for all my transportation for four years before I could afford to buy another car," Rick said.

The car was a 1936 Ford coupe. Time being on the precipice of the '50's, it brought two hundred and fifty dollars. Twenty-one months after baby Steven was born he required ten days of hospitalization in a private room. The total medical cost was five hundred dollars.

In those early days of their marriage they lived in Muncie, and Rick worked for Ball Brothers (glass jars). His pay for a 48-hour week was thirty-two dollars. The biggest paycheck he ever earned there was seventy dollars, and that was for working a double shift.

Window boxes were still in vogue, and the couple had one on the shady side of the house. Trouble was it didn't keep the baby's formula from spoiling. Those were the days when all kinds of household goods were offered for sale at a dollar down and a dollar a week.

Rick and Betty bought a Philco refrigerator on those terms and were awarded a bonus, a free Philco radio. When they arrived home there was a pink notice in the mailbox for Rick. He was laid off. Luckily, the lay-off lasted only two days, the only two days he was unemployed in his life.

Rick was fifteen when he first declared a deep affection for Betty. He sang solos at church and predictably had attracted some girls at Sunday School. When they concocted a note asking him which of them he liked best he informed Betty, "I don't want any of them. I'd rather have you."

The second time he revealed his love for her was down in Tennessee.

"I was home on furlough from the Army," Rick recalled. "Her mother had been sick and she expressed a desire to die where she was born, in Tennessee, and they had moved down there.

"I drove down there and Betty was out in the barn milking," he recalled. "She didn't see me coming, so I stood on one side of the cow while she milked on the other, and I struck up a conversation with her. She had no idea who was talking with her. When she stood up and saw me she almost dropped the bucket of milk. She was tickled to death to see me."

His next step remains memorably gallant. "I went and asked her dad if it would be all right to marry Betty," he said, savoring the recollection with obvious feeling. "Her dad said 'Yes,' and he said, 'Myrtle,'— that was Betty's mother, and she had died – he said, 'Myrtle would have liked that, too.' Being as Betty was under age we went up to Dalton, Georgia, and we got married there. Her dad drove us."

Literally hundreds of boys and adult males in several states may remember Rick. From 1964 through

**Richard and Betty Jackson**

1974 he held the position of ranger at Boy Scout Camp Redwing, at Muncie, and from 1974 until his retirement in 1995 he was Camp Ranger at Ransburg Reservation on Lake Monroe, near Bloomington. A few days before this writing the last of a summer's 3,200 scouts (500 more than the previous year) had said so-long to him after a fun week at the popular 624-acre Cross Roads of America Boy Scout campground in southeastern Monroe County.

For the first couple of years after they arrived there Betty acted as camp nurse, and the boys called her "Mom." But for many years she spent summers as daytime gate attendant at the Paynetown Recreation Area, at Lake Monroe, and became known by her own name to countless lake patrons.

Rick and Betty were approaching fifty years together, and had yet to have their first serious argument. And after that first experience with the refrigerator, they never purchased anything else on time payments. Moreover, when she got a job they never bought a thing that couldn't be covered by Rick's paycheck. After Steven two more children were born to them, Shirley, and Richard Mark. They also had seven grandkids, a pet dog named "Zipper," and two outside watchdogs.

With the boy scouts gone for the season and Ransburg returned to its usual late summer inactivity, you'd think the camp ranger would be ready for a vacation. But Rick expressed a couple interesting thoughts on that subject.

First of all, everything and anything it took to maintain a camp the size of Ransburg had to be tended to. Fifty-five acres of grass still needed mowing. There were also the demands of waiting boat repairs, building repairs, plumbing repairs and electrical work.

Then, too, there was the need to get things ready for the next summer.

"I haven't taken a vacation in years," Rick went on. "People travel hundreds of miles to see what I see here every day. There are seven miles of shoreline here, making swimming, sailing and canoeing all available to me. We're surrounded by nature. The sounds we hear are birds singing, and the wind in the trees. You look around and you see foxes, quails, turkeys, coyotes. You look up and you see the sky, the clouds, the sun. At night you see the stars. It's quiet. When you're out here you're in God's cathedral. What more could we want?" he asked.

# TRAPPED IN A KEYHOLE

Cissy Sullivan didn't go to school on Monday.

The curly haired, brown-eyed six-year-old had a sore finger.

It got caught in a lock, in a filling station, and it was too sore to go to school with.

It happened on a Sunday evening, when Cissy and her brother Robbie went to the filling station to use the pay phone to call Cissy's adopted mother to come get them.

While twelve year old Robbie dialed the number, Cissy toyed with the knob of a door in the filling station. Then she stuck her finger in the keyhole – and couldn't get it out.

Robbie tried to free Cissy's finger, but he couldn't get it out either.

The man at the filling station also tried to get Cissy's finger out of the keyhole, but he couldn't.

It looked like Cissy was trapped in the keyhole for life.

The man at the filling station called an ambulance.

Then he set about taking the lock off the door.

When the ambulance arrived the EMTs took Cissy and the keyhole – and the door lock – to Bloomington Hospital.

There the emergency room personnel got Cissy's finger out of its prison.

Cissy was well pleased with the work of the people at the hospital. While still trapped in the keyhole at the filling station, she figured her finger would have to be cut off before she could be freed.

"I was scared to death," she said.

When her foster parents, James and Ann Sullivan, had her back home that Sunday night, Cissy had some advice for them.

"Don't ever put your finger in a lock," she warned, "or you'll get caught."

Now you know why Cissy didn't go to school on Monday.

# THE WORKPLACE

Few workplaces have been blessed with natural scenery as was the little building that housed Wesley Martin's. In a splendor of burgeoning fall color, maple and oak trees outside its front door rose from a still-green incline to touch a glassy blue October sky.

Majestic sycamore, stalwart poplar and oak, and spreading maple swayed and rustled their bewitching hues in a woodsy area at its rear. There was no entrance there.

At the sides of the structure were roughly shaped mortarless stone-walled planters, placed there by some unprofessional yet coarsely talented hand, and a collection of autumn colors bloomed beautifully there too. A county blacktop ran past the front door, and a gravel drive circled around the back.

The building was painted white with green trim around its front door and its two small side windows. In the front gable point someone had tacked a clock whose face was as big around as a dinner plate. There were numbers on the face – from one to twelve – but no hands. The gable point was so near to the ground a tall man could probably have reached up and placed his own hands on the clock.

Inside the building the same man might have had to hunch to keep from cracking his head on the ceiling. Lying flat on his back on the floor in one direction he'd have had to bend his knees to fit. If he lay on the floor in the other direction his head would have hung out the door.

A tall man. Not Martin. He was average height, enviously paunchless, and at sixty-five favored by fortune with a head of thick iron-gray hair shaped in a handsome bur. However else he might have wanted to do it, he would have fit into the place. But it was not necessary that he should have lain on the floor.

Crammed in his workplace were two well-worn overstuffed chairs, side by side against the back wall; also two metal chairs folded against a side wall, an operating electric baseboard heater, two built-in shelves for holding magazines or newspapers, a radio and a small television. The top shelf made a kind of corner table and was covered by a piece of oilcloth. Martin's wife had covered it one day to improve the looks of the place.

On one unpainted wall there was a living color newspaper photo of Heltonville's revered son, Damon Bailey, in basketball action at his last game with Indiana University. On the opposite wall there was a huge calendar with extra large appointment squares for each day. Protruding from the wall above Bailey's photo was a large white electric bulb ballooning from a white porcelain socket.

Near the ceiling in a corner of that same wall there was a newspaper clipping. It was not a story about Bailey, nor was it a story about basketball, or Indiana University. It was a story about Lawrence County dumpsters and Lawrence County dumping.

It was not surprising that it should be there, for

Martin's workplace, however blessed, was the county dumpsite near Heltonville.  He was a caretaker there.

When open, his door looked out across the blacktop to sixteen tall and short box-like green dumpsters all in a row at the foot of the grassy incline.  One contained aluminum cans.  Another, newspapers.  Each had an open lock dangling from it.  Martin smiled when asked about the locks, and he said, "Yes, cans have been stolen from that bin.  But they only took the cans that were in bags.  They didn't touch the loose ones, or the newspapers."

Until caretakers were hired to oversee public dumping, dumpsites such as the one near Heltonville were an incredible mess.  More trash and refuse was dumped on the ground than in the tall green bins.

"It must have been bad," Martin said.  "The truck drivers say there was so much trash on the ground they couldn't drive the trucks to the dumpsters to load them.  Not anymore.  We see that is not done anymore.  You see how clean this place is.  But you still have to watch," he shook his head.  "There are people who would dump on the ground if you didn't watch them."

Martin was retired and worked at the dumpsite as a part-timer.  His hours were unusual and few people would care to work them.  He was on the job two days a week, Saturday and Sunday, from 6 a.m. till 10 p.m.  It was not the most lucrative job, but the money helped pay for Martin's medicines.

Although there were magazines and old newspapers on the two shelves inside the green-trimmed white shelter, Martin rarely had a chance to enjoy them on his long weekends there.

"The minute you try to read, here comes someone to dump trash, and you have to go out to watch," he said.

"You might get a chance to talk to someone, but there's no chance to read here."

Sitting on what Martin called the "patio" was a bonus that went with the caretaker's job. On nice days he placed the two metal folding chairs outside on the blacktop. Sometimes a visitor occupied the second chair. And thanks to a big light that illuminated the entire dumpsite, the patio was also available to Martin at night.

The overstuffed chairs, metal folding chairs, and all the furnishings inside the small building, came from the long row of tall green bins across the blacktop. So did the clock with no hands.

"Everything in this place was a throw-away," Martin said. "Even the television," he indicated the small set on the oil cloth-covered shelf. "But all we can get is Channel 11, and that's not too good."

Situated on the back side of Heltonville and seemingly remote from everything else, the location of the dumpsite offered someone an opportunity to play a trick on Martin one night.

"I came to work one morning and when I unlocked the padlock and pulled on the door to open it, it fell off," he said. "During the night someone had removed the screws from the hinges."

As the door fell outward the hasp raked painfully across the back of Martin's hand, but he was otherwise unhurt. He was a sport about it.

"Probably just some boys having fun," he shrugged with a smile.

# LIBERTY

He didn't look old enough to be dead, this boy, this warrior, "this tabernacle," as the minister referred to him later.

He had a shock of rusty hair over a handsome sleeping face. From a gleaming brass-buttoned blue tunic a military collar rose high around his neck.

Cpl. Rickey Dale Southern, twenty years old, had been killed in action in the Vietnam War.

That's what the newspapers had written a week earlier.

He was dead.

Now he was home and those words were written in tears on the faces of his loved ones.

They were etched on the blue, red and gold of the Marine Corps Honor Guard as they sat rigid, eyes front, white caps held in white-gloved hands.

Standing before the bier, Rev. C. A. Lattimer said, "There is no doubt in our minds today that Rickey lived up to the oath that he took, that he paid the greatest price to keep this great country of ours free from Godless oppression."

A couple of blocks west of the Greene and Harrell Funeral Home in downtown Bloomington, free

46

Americans went about their usual Saturday afternoon shopping on Courthouse Square.

Down in Atlanta the Reds and the Braves had just begun to play ball.

The annual Kentucky Derby was only hours away.

The minister continued: "In God's name, let us respect those who have given their very lives for us . . . the dear cost of our liberty that we hold so close . . ."

Semper Fidelis.

So help me God.

More than a quarter of a century of service to the Corps shone bright and gold from the sleeves of the Honor Guard. Medals and ribbons from campaigns of World War II to Vietnam glittered on their chests.

Scores of mourners filled the funeral home to standing room only. Floral pieces covered what remaining space was left.

There were family, friends, classmates, and some who came to mourn a boy-stranger, Monroe County's first casualty of the war in Vietnam.

They stood outside on the sidewalk and watched the Marines carry Rickey's flag-draped casket to the waiting hearse.

Traffic on East Kirkwood Avenue slowed, then stopped as the long procession moved slowly behind a city police escort toward Knightridge Cemetery, in Salt Creek Township.

From the Halls of Montezuma.

Back at the funeral home the organist had played "America." As always it was music to rouse the emotions. It brought more tears.

The long line of cars moved slowly.

A small boy straddled his stopped bicycle and stared.

Cars stopped at every intersection.

Up ahead, riding with the driver of the hearse was

Cpl. Thomas Sullivan, twenty-two, of Philadelphia. He had been with the flag-covered casket since its arrival in Philadelphia.

This was Cpl. Sullivan's twenty-sixth body escort detail. Twenty-five of those he brought home were Marines younger than himself. One was two months older.

Also toward the front of the procession, in two Marine Corps vehicles, the Honor Guard was made up of ten Marine recruiters under the command of M/Sgt. Russell Murray of Indianapolis. It was their job to fill the ranks of the Corps . . . and their duty to be where they were now when a fallen comrade came home.

An anxious motorist cut into the procession on East Third Street and then left a block later.

Two girls walking with the green light at the Ind. 46 by-pass were halted by the ever-moving procession.

A motorcyclist darted in and out of the line as he passed first one car and then another.

"Look beyond this hour of sorrow . . . ," Rev. Lattimer said at the cemetery.

On a knoll north of the young warrior's final resting place rifle-bearing Marines in dress uniforms stood at parade rest.

Gently, hands which once knew mortal combat folded the flag. In military fashion it was presented to Cpl. Sullivan.

"In the name of this great country of ours . . . ," the young Marine presented it to the family.

Three volleys of rifle fire rent the overcast sky, startling mourners..

A distant bugle sounded Taps.

Farewell.

"Death is swallowed up in victory," the minister said.

**Rickey Dale Southern**

Riflemen stood at present arms.

The Honor Guard stiffened in final salute.

Muted sobs accented the melancholy notes; tears streamed down a dozen cheeks.

Suddenly it was over.

All that remained was a damp chill in the afternoon air. And the body of a boy.

A warrior.

"This tabernacle," the minister had said, "whose soul we leave in Your hands."

# THE SECTION HAND

Where you think you ought to find a man when you go to visit him and where you do find him can be a traumatic experience. Take my visit one winter day to the home of Robert S. Wright in Switz City.

When I learned that Mr. Wright had attained his ninetieth year, which is no small feat, and I had decided to pay him a call, it would not have surprised me to have found him resting comfortably by the fire.

In my years of interviewing the elderly I have learned that many of them, perhaps most, age that way in the winter time. A few times I have found them in wheelchairs, or bedfast. But Mr. Wright was totally different from all of them. So, where did I find him? In his backyard pushing snow off the path that led from the back door of his house to the outhouse.

So help me.

Fearing a heart attack many younger men would not have dared do what he was doing.

Mr. Wright was wearing rubbers over his shoes, an insulated jacket, and a fuzzy hat with ear-flaps, the strings of which were undone and flopping. He looked for all the world to me like an overgrown kid, and with those flopping ear-flaps he reminded me of a big coon dog romping in the season's first snowfall, and smiling like either or both.

51

"I don't need to be out here," he laughed an unnecessary apology to me.

He didn't. He had a modern bathroom in the neat white frame that was his home. "But," he added with another laugh, "I ain't no 'count for anything." And gesturing toward the old, gray privy, he pshawed, "I don't use that thing anymore. I just cleaned off the walk so I can carry my trash back there."

The trauma I suffered at finding Mr. Wright where I found him, doing what he was doing there, wiped my mind of the many questions I had planned to ask him. But I learned some things I might not have had I remembered them. For example, he seemed anxious for me to know, he got saved when he was forty-nine.

"I used to drink and smoke," he told me. "And cuss – ! Why, ever' time I opened my mouth I'd cuss. And I used to smoke cigars, pipe, cigarettes – anything I could get my hands on. And," he smiled at the recollection, "I'd chew a plug o' tobacco a day. Why, I'd walk out of church and before the door could close behind me I'd be stuffin' a chew in my mouth. And I drunk whiskey and beer ever' day. Then," he raised a hand in cleaver-like fashion and let it fall, "I chopped it off right now. And I never touched any of it anymore. And I stopped the cussin' too."

I recalled my own withdrawal problems when I had quit smoking, how I craved cigarettes for months afterwards . . . the muscle spasms that would nearly knock me out of a chair, or bed . . . the sleepless nights . . . the nicotine fits. And I asked Mr. Wright about his difficulties after he quit so many bad habits at once.

"I never did have no trouble," he said. "The Lord come to me. He took the desire for all that away from me. And I never did want anymore."

I thought about the millions of hopes and dollars

spent each year on unsuccessful nicotine and alcohol cures, and I said aloud: "You're putting me on."

And Mr. Wright said, "No!" And his voice rose slightly in pitch, as older people will do when they become solicitous, sincere. "No!" he repeated. "That happened." And he shook his head and smiled with satisfaction. "Yes, sir! It did!"

My next question failed to elicit the answer I'd hoped to hear, at least not entirely.

"Oh, yes," he said. "Since I got saved I've felt better. I'd say it helped my body, my nerves and maybe it helped me all over. But," he laughed, "I just wonder why I have lived this long too. I never imagined – his voice once again rose in pitch – that I'd live to be ninety years old."

Thinking then that the secret to his longevity could perhaps have been in his diet, Mr. Wright, in answer to my question said: "Oh, for breakfast I'll have cereals, or apple pie, maybe peach pie; and always two cups of coffee.

"At dinnertime," he went on, "I'll eat beans – on light bread. Sometimes on cornbread. I'll have gravy a lot o' the time. And at supper – well, I eat hardly anything at supper. A cup of warm milk and bread. Jello! I eat a lot of Jello. I'll eat some bacon some, and some boiled meat and taters. But not much," he said.

He retired early – between 8:30 and 10:00 P.M. And, he said, "I don't get up 'till eight o'clock in the morning, and," incredibly, he added with emphasis, "I sleep all that time."

He liked television "pretty well" and "I just look at all of it," he said. But he had a favorite show – Hee Haw. "I like Hee Haw," he said. "I like it pretty well. And I look at them about regular."

Mr. Wright had five living children in the surrounding area who visited him regularly. He spoke of a sixth – a son, Gerald Wayne Wright.

"He stayed in the Navy twenty-seven years then took a heart attack one day and died."

Lillie, the mother of his children, was also dead.

In earlier days, Mr. Wright was a section hand for the Pennsylvania Railroad, and for the Illinois Central. He also was a farmer. And to keep his thumb green he put out a garden every summer. He looked at a spading fork whose rusted tines were a sharp contrast to the white snow from which they rose to a weathered working handle in the garden area.

"I put out a few cabbages, mangos, carrots, lettuce, and sweet corn out there, and some other things."

I tried to measure the garden space with my eyes. "Pretty big, isn't it? Looks like it'd take a lot of work," I said.

Mr. Wright smiled, nodded his head, and then said in a burst of unashamed candor, "It did for me! Yeh!"

A sudden impulse struck me and I wanted to put a friendly arm around his shoulders. Instead I just laughed with him and steered him back to a less burdensome memory.

"About that smoking, chewing, drinking and cussing," I said, "Would you advise smokers, chewers, drinkers and cussers to quit?"

He smiled a broad smile.

"All of them," he said. "I advise all of them to quit. Not because I belong to the church, but because all that is not good for anybody."

As we carefully picked our way over the newly shoveled but still slippery path that led across the grass from the outhouse to the house, and then to the gate in the white picket fence beyond which I had parked my car, Mr. Wright spoke again.

"Be careful," he solicitously cautioned me. "Don't slip and fall."

# ROMA

When she was a teacher Roma Wilson once had trouble in class with a popular but crude expression of the time: "Shut up."

To discourage it she installed a classroom cuss box and levied a penny penalty every time the phrase was spoken. It initially worked well enough so that she tried it with her five children at home. Before it could prove itself there she made a couple of damaging errors.

1) The project fell apart at school because she used the penalty money to buy bubble gum for her pupils. "They began saying things deliberately then, just to get bubble gum," she said.

2) The cuss box failed at home because of . . . guess who? One day the off-duty teacher turned to one of her noisy children and in exasperation exclaimed, "Shut up!"

Roma taught at Sandwich, Ill, Union Mills, Ind., and wound up her career at Spencer. At Union Mills, snow days were made up on Saturdays. That wasn't so bad because Saturday make-up days were always followed by Saturday night dances.

"The trustee felt sorry for us," she said, and added,

"We had a lot of fun at Union Mills. We had four rooms in the high school and each teacher knew every pupil by name, and their parents. We walked to school then and when it snowed, those of us who could get there would all gather in one room."

She never spanked or paddled, and never sent a kid to the principal's office. "But," she threw back her head and rolled her eyes as she remembered, "I sure did want to shake a few of them."

She had a couple methods for controlling trouble-makers. One was a finger in the shoulder, always administered with a pleasant smile and gentle words. The kids had a name for the other method:

"Clipping."

It worked surprisingly well. Speaking sweetly, she'd back a tough guy to a wall and, smiling all the while, tenderly chuck him under the chin. The move always came as a surprise and invariably the young man would jerk his head back.

Boink!

That method never broke a wall but the trouble-maker was suddenly wide-eyed, respectful, and eager to listen to teacher.

Impressive?

A new boy was once warned, "Look out for Mrs. Wilson, she'll clip yuh."

In her sitting room at her Spencer home one after-noon, Roma didn't appear to be that threatening. Approaching her eighty-seventh birthday, she was certainly feisty, but amusingly self-deprecating, and enviably slim and refreshing as a model for a break-fast cereal commercial.

"I was a failure at everything I did," she laughed at herself and related a story of earlier days as a home-ec teacher.

"We were in the cooking lab and needed to heat a can of pork and beans," she began. "At home we always put cans down in hot water. At school that day I put the can in the oven. When it got hot it exploded and blew up the stove. We had pork and beans splattered all over the walls."

Once she heard a boy whisper that his mother was coming to school to "Take care of Mrs. Wilson." When the woman arrived and demanded to know what her son had done to deserve two F's on his report card, Mrs. Wilson replied, "Nothing."

When I asked her to recount her best experience as a teacher she was just as brief. "Retirement," she said.

"They may not have learned anything," she said of the many kids who passed through her classrooms, "but I tried to teach them."

This is not the first time she's had her name in print. The daughter of an Evangelical minister whose parents were a Catholic mother and a Baptist father, she was born in Pleasant City, Ohio. "When I was born," she explained, "there was an article in the paper about my great grandfather being the oldest person in town, and I the youngest."

She studied at church colleges in Naperville, Ill., and at Evansville, Ind. During her career she took time off to have five children.

"Five wonderful children," she said of an attentive family that lived near enough to lunch with or visit her regularly.

Roma also was a church organist for thirty years. She would have liked singing in the choir, too.

"But," she complained, "I didn't have a voice."

She recalled that after she did sing with the choir one Sunday the director observed, "Now I know why you play the organ, Roma."

Eye surgery forced her to give up the organ. At her retirement the choir director thanked her and added, "You weren't very good, Roma, but you were faithful."

Roma rocked back in her chair and laughed and clapped her hands at the memory.

"My parents gave me elocution, piano and organ lessons, but I wasn't good at anything," she said feigning sorrow.

But she was capable of programming her own VCR.

Before her surgery she played piano at nursing homes and the organ at a funeral home. She also enjoyed riding a bicycle. Her insurance agent saw her riding her bike on the sidewalk one day and was shocked.

"He kept saying, 'I can't believe it, I can't believe it.' He couldn't believe that an old lady like me would be riding a bicycle," Roma said.

"It was all so much fun," she said whimsically of her past. She shrugged off the thought as suddenly as it had come and she smiled, "Now I crochet. It keeps me off the sidewalks, I suppose."

# THE WAY THEY WERE

You probably didn't know him, and maybe you have never heard of him. But when I ran the stars and stripes up the flagpole in our yard one day I got thinking about Bill Collins. The occasion was Veterans Day, Friday, Nov. 11.

Collins always knew it as Armistice Day. The name was derived from World War I, and Collins was a Doughboy in that war. It was changed to Veterans Day in later years to honor all those who served in this country's wars.

He had little argument with that, but when Congress in 1968 moved Veterans Day up to the fourth Monday in October to give federal employees another three-day weekend, guys like Collins protested. Americans in general joined them; they just couldn't buy the change. They ignored it through their silence and lack of participation.

State legislatures quickly changed back to the Nov. 11 holiday. Except for federal employees the new Veterans Day was meaningless. It took five years to get the attention of Congress, and Veterans Day was moved back to Nov. 11, effective on that date in 1978.

When all the veterans have gone to their eternal

reward somebody in Washington may again try to make a long weekend holiday out of that date. And the move may be successful. To date, however, no one there has been foolhardy enough to monkey with it, even though Collins and a lot of veterans like him are no longer here to protest.

Nov. 11 was really their day. Despite the name change, to them it was always Armistice Day. The years of my boyhood were highlighted by parades on that holiday. And as Collins and the men and women who were in service with him during World War I preferred to do, I too look on Nov. 11 as Armistice Day. When I've thought of accepting the new name a visit I had with Collins many years ago pertaining to the first Armistice Day comes to mind.

It is one of my top few war stories and my all-time favorite. I had heard many stories of all kinds before my meeting with Collins, and many more since then. Few have affected me as having been so rich in the touching simplicity of family love, and I was, and still am, deeply moved by it. It's a very short story, and I hope it will inspire some of you to send me your favorite war story.

"Both sides was afightin' as hard as they could, right up to 11 o'clock that day, then they shut it off like a switch," is the way Collins began telling me of what happened in his sector of trench warfare that memorable day in 1918.

"We built fires to keep warm by that night," he continued. "We didn't care to, but they said it'd be all right. And it was. In a couple days we got word that an armistice had been signed, and that the war was over."

He recalled the mood of the men in the 151st Infantry of the Indiana 38th Division.

"We doubted there was an armistice," he recalled. "There was no celebration, no big to-do. We just wanted to go home."

After a delousing at Brest, France, he sailed for the U.S. On his arrival he was discharged and given train fare to Bloomington. Because I was unprepared for the direction his story would take, I was suddenly and inadvertently caught up in the emotion of it.

"I come up to Bloomington from Louisville on the old Monon," he was saying. "Got here about 11:30 at night. It was just unbelievable that I was here. My family didn't know I was comin' home. Communications wasn't like they are now. They thought I was still in France. I got a taxi. A Model-T Ford. And I paid six dollars to get from Bloomington to where we had our farm a couple o'miles west of Little Cincinnati, in Greene County."

Collins, a tall, large man with blue eyes and a head thick with white hair, hesitated to run a hand over his mouth. He was chewing tobacco and while he talked he would periodically spit into an empty, rusted Hi-C can. But, unknown to me because I was busy writing in my notebook, he'd taken that time not really to swipe at his mouth but to give himself a few moments to get a hold on his emotions.

"When I got out o' the taxi there at home," he went on with his narrative, "and I started walking up t'the house, I gave a 'Hello-o-o-o.' And in the dark night I heard my father's voice asayin' to my mother, 'Get up Vine . . .'"

Collins hadn't got as good a hold on his emotions as he'd hoped, for he choked up at the memory and that is when I realized that something was happening. The big man was overcome with feeling. I could almost sense the weight of his thoughts at that moment.

"He said . . . ," Collins was making an attempt at continuing his story. He couldn't. He paused, then he tried again. And this time he got it out.

"I heard my dad say, 'Get up Vine, Bill's home.'"

Again Collins was quiet, unable to speak. His jaw bulged and fell as he shifted the chew of tobacco. He rubbed his hand over his mouth again. When he was able he spoke again.

"There wasn't no huggin' or kissin' or nothin' like some does," he said softly. "My father and mother just asked how I was. Then just set down at the kitchen table and talked till about seven in the morning. That's the way we was."

# SILVER LODE

Two best friends were walking down the street. "If you could have any wish," one asked, "what would it be?"

"A mountain of gold," replied the other.

Said the first man: "You surely would give me half, wouldn't you?"

"I would not," said the other firmly. "Not an ounce."

His friend was deeply hurt. "What!" he demanded. "All these years of friendship and this is what I get?"

"Look," said the other as he turned and started walking in the opposite direction, "wish yourself your own mountain of gold and leave mine alone."

Being a better best friend than that, I will share a treasure with you. This one's in a story, too, a legend, really, and of doubtful authenticity, but it'll probably be as close as you'll ever come to a mountain of gold. So, lean back and listen to what I have to say.

When Indians roamed southcentral Indiana there lived in Martin County a man named Absalom Fields. One day he was surprised by a small band of

Choctaw Indians who lived in Mitchelltree Township near Dover Hill and Trinity. Fields was certain he would be killed and scalped. But he was happily mistaken.

"We no hurt you," their leader assured Fields. "We take you and show you something."

He was thereupon blindfolded, turned around, placed in a boat and paddled up or down the East Fork of White River. Eventually Fields was guided into a deep cave in a mammoth sandstone outcropping now known as McBride's Bluffs. When the blindfold was at last removed he was standing before a larger gathering of Indians. Between them on the ground was a veritible treasure – a stack of silver bullion.

Beginning to sound like a television script? Check it out. It is not totally my story. While some of it was told to me, some of it can be found in a "History of Martin County," written by the late Harry Q. Holt, onetime superintendent of schools. It can be found at the public library at Shoals.

There is no known reason for the unusual confidence extended Fields. But shortly thereafter the Indians moved west, leaving behind the silver and a white man sick with silver fever. W.E. McBride, an early owner of the land on which the ancient sandstone outcropping is situated, left a yellowing writing pertaining to Fields's impassioned search for the fortune in silver bars.

"All his life (Fields) would hunt the hills between Indian Creek and the river. But he could never find the cave. His sons Joseph, William and George would hunt the same ground, but they could never find it," he had written for posterity.

Quoting Fields, McBride described the silver bars

as having been "three quarters of an inch to three and four inches wide, and six, to seven, to eight inches long" and stacked in a "rick."

After years of retelling this story the treasure in silver grew to include nuggets of gold. This led to at least one phony claim to the fortune. According to legend, a stranger rode into Martin County one day and identified himself as William Henry, the husband of the daughter of a Choctaw Indian chief. Henry said he was sent by the Indians to retrieve the "golden nuggets." In his history, Holt estimates the height of McBride's Bluff at one hundred seventy-five feet. From the river below, it seemed less. Yet, some have guessed the height to be two hundred. From the river road that runs past there, a search of the ponderous sandstone outcropping with a telephoto lens revealed no opening in which the treasure might have been hidden. Nor was there, through the density of green foliage, any sign of three tell-tale symbols – a half moon, a star and a snake, allegedly chiseled somewhere on the vast facing – that are said to mark the location of the cave.

A "colonel of Indiana volunteers" returned to Bedford after the Civil War to tell of a Tennesseean who had made numerous trips to Indiana before the war to trade with Indians. He was supposed to have related how a band of them was encountered on the banks of the White River "near large bluffs." And from a secret place within the bluffs they produced "silver bars, and trinkets made of silver," which they traded to the white men.

A man named Joe Norman claimed to have found the half moon and star symbols, but not that of the snake, pointing to the possibility that the three are chiseled in places separated by great distances.

Mark McBride, in 1890, claimed to have found all three, but not the treasure.

Down through the years many people have searched McBride's Bluffs for the rick of silver bars. It is said that the fortune is still in a cave there. Before you start spending your share of that treasure I must, as a friend, also tell you this. According to Holt some Indians debarked from a train at Shoals one day in 1910 and presumably made their way to McBride's Bluffs. They were later seen returning to the train depot carrying on their shoulders a heavily bound blanket suspended from a pole. They boarded a westbound train and were never seen again.

# FRIENDS

She had lived a long time. Maybe too long, for she had sighed to her good friend a year earlier, "Almost all of my friends are gone, now."

For people of her generation, that was not an uncommon thing to say, especially on Thanksgiving Day, or Christmas, or Easter. It was traditional for people of her age on those days to count their blessings, if they had any, and not television sporting events.

Her generation had come to life more than eight decades earlier. One of the last to leave it, she was called away at age eighty-four. In whatever way one may choose to tally the years, she had lived a long time. Despite that, a journalist on the obit desk was clever enough to sum up her time on earth in five short paragraphs. The shortest was a paragraph in which her survivors were listed – two, a relative by marriage and a good friend.

The funeral home from which she was buried was kind; viewing hours were as liberal for her last hours on earth as they had been even for the popular and the distinguished who had preceded her there. Sixteen persons came during those hours, including the good friend, a reporter, and the minister retained to preach her funeral. Counting the minister there were six people at the service. Some of those were body bearers.

There might have been more people in attendance, but another Thanksgiving Day was only hours away and, coming in the middle of the week as it does, who could have taken the time? In her day it was different; having a funeral on a holiday or on a weekend was a virtual guarantee of a sizeable turnout of mourners, and some curious. But times had changed. She had lived long enough to learn that holidays and weekends are not for funerals but for fun and games. She should have picked a more convenient time to die.

"She was a very sweet old lady, always willing to help people," her good friend, a younger lady, speaking in hushed tones, put a spoken addition to the brief obit that had appeared in the paper. "She saw no wrong in anybody that she knew, and I never heard her speak wrong of anyone in the time I knew her."

Ironically their friendship had begun near another Thanksgiving Day fifteen Novembers earlier.

"She lived on the floor above me in the Allen Building on E. Kirkwood, in Bloomington," the good friend began recounting the seeds of that friendship. "She found out that I had fallen and broken my leg and began helping me. She'd come down at six-thirty in the morning and fix my breakfast. Then she'd do for me until she'd tuck me in at nine o'clock, when she'd go back upstairs."

After a few moments of silence during which the good friend nodded her head several times as older folks will do when overcome by the profundity of simple words, she added, "She did for me every single day for twelve whole weeks."

Thanksgiving Day that year had come early in those

twelve weeks. The two women had enjoyed a bountiful day, just the two of them, and they spoke of many things. Afterwards, Thanksgiving Day seemed to extend itself to every day in the subsequent months and years.

When she spoke those words, "Almost all my friends are gone now," on the last Thanksgiving Day of her life, she was one of thirteen persons who had gathered in the apartment of her good friend.

"She sat on the davenport and had a nice dinner." the good friend remembered.

It was just a matter of days after that when the good friend found herself repaying some of the devotion shown her during those twelve weeks of care.

"She got sick," she continued her soft-spoken memory of the woman lying so still in the casket. "She liked a cookie for breakfast, and I'd take her some. After I had a stroke I couldn't go to her but once a week, because I had dizzy spells. On one of those visits she got very serious and she asked if I'd take over when she died.

"She said, 'I don't have anybody.'

"I told her that I would. She arranged to leave me enough money to pay for her funeral. That's what I did. When she died I called the funeral home. I was sick, so a man came to my house and we sat at the kitchen table and made all the arrangements."

After a while the good friend began speaking in little sighing tones as elderly people sometimes do when they're sad and pained.

"There she was," she said in weighted yet almost inaudible tones, "without chick or child. Dead."

There was another silence. Then still dry-eyed and composed the woman spoke again.

"She never would take a penny's pay for those

twelve weeks. Then, when I was tending to her she'd say, 'You shouldn't come up here. Don't come up here. You're not able.' She was so good. Such a sweet person."

The younger woman then took some solace from another act of kindness she had extended to her friend two months before the older woman's death.

"I took her to the nursing home and paid out of my own purse  to get her settled there," she said.

This true account of friends was included here to induce readers to remember the elderly, especially one who at this moment may be thinking, "I don't have anybody."

# TOM BROWN'S DOGS

Tom Brown had buried his big red setter. He hadn't wanted to do that, but the dog was dead. Hit by a car. Tom said the animal had lived overnight, and that he really didn't expect he'd survive the mishap that long. But the dog did. At least Tom thought it did. Anyway, Red – that was the dog's name – was dead when Tom checked on him the next morning.

Tom buried him near the dog's favorite drinking place – Indian Creek. It runs through the farm that Tom managed: the Luther Ferguson place on Indiana 58 between Blue Hole and Wagner Pond, not far from Springville. A stranger might find the place if he knew it was about a mile north of the Greene-Lawrence county line.

There were five hundred acres there. Before Luther acquired it, a man by the name of Roscoe Wagner owned it, hence the name Wagner's Pond for a dried up water hole on the farm. Tom, who was sixty-eight at this time, managed the whole thing. And from what his friends said of him, he worked from daylight to dark every day, hitting it just as hard as any young man could.

Tom agreed: "Sometimes, two hours out of every twenty-four I don't do anything but sleep," he said.

Once, a long time ago, his wife, Zetta, appeared in one of my newspaper columns after I'd knocked on their door in search of something to write. I sometimes did that. Knocked on a strange door just to see what I'd come up with. Got some pretty interesting columns that way. Tom, who was out in the fields during my visit with Zetta, later expressed his opinion of that column in these words: "You should have talked with me."

Tom had a great deal of affection for Red, or maybe it was respect. It didn't matter to him that some people derogatorily referred to Red as, "One of those big, long-haired, red dogs that runs and slobbers all over the place." Red had done some great things, and Tom preferred to remember them, not the inherited nervous traits of the Irish setter.

Could be that's why he put a plate of dog food by Red's grave, there on Indian Creek. "If he gets hungry," Tom said as though he expected Red might one day rise from the dead, "he'll have something to eat."

Red was one of those kinds of dogs that tagged along after Tom wherever his master went. That meant that Tom wanted it that way, too. When Tom was behind the wheel of his pickup, Red was sitting straight up in the bed. If Tom took a notion to go bird hunting, Red was right there to lend his assistance.

Red was probably the greatest bird dog that ever stood on point. A few days after the loss of his canine friend, Tom, wearing a red billed cap, overalls and gum boots during a visit to the general store in town, was eulogizing the animal. And he told of their remarkable first hunt together.

"I was carrying a single-shot 12-gauge behind Red when he went on point, standing part way in a brush pile," Tom remembered. "When I called out 'flush' to him I noticed that he moved back a little, and at about the same time a quail flew up. I expected a whole covey to come up, but I aimed, fired and got the one bird anyway.

"After I reloaded I noticed that Red was still on point, standing kind of in that brush pile, so I got all ready again and I said 'flush' again," he continued. "Sure enough, Red kind of stepped back a little and another bird flew up. I shot him and reloaded. And there was Red, still standing midway into that brush pile, on point again.

"Well sir," Tom said, "after Red had flushed five birds, and I brought them all down, a single shot at the time, I stepped over to that brush pile to see what was going on. I could hardly believe what I saw!

"Red had trapped a whole covey of quail in a ground-hog hole by holding a front paw over the opening!" The look on Tom's face was one of incredulity as he continued to explain. "Each time I said 'flush' he had raised that paw and let one bird out. I'll tell you, that dog didn't only know birds, he also knew shotguns."

Tom paused a few moments then went on: "Old Red had a serious handicap," he said almost sadly. "He was deaf. But he found a way to overcome it, he learned to read lips."

If you ignore the fact that they'd met with fatal and strange circumstances, Tom had had some pretty good dogs in his time. Not the least of which was Jack, a large coon dog who, Tom claimed, not only ran coons but also slew and brought them home to fit pre-cut pelt-boards.

"Why, that dog would see me whittling a board and just take off right now," Tom said. "And pretty soon here he'd come, dragging in a coon to fit it. Big or small board, it wouldn't matter, old Jack would bring in a coon to fit it.

"One day, a few years back," he went on with a shake of his head, "Zetta, my wife, was ironing in the kitchen and she opened the door to let in some fresh air. Jack happened to be going past at the time and he looked in.

"Well," Tom said, his voice beginning to take on a tone of wonderment, "Jack saw that ironing board and he took off, and I haven't seen hide nor hair of him since! He's still out there someplace looking for a coon big enough to fit that ironing board."

Tom never gave up on Jack. He believed the dog would not disappoint him, that Jack would one day show up with a coon large enough to fit Zetta's ironing board.

"Yes sir," Tom said emphatically. "He's just that good of a coon dog."

With Jack on a prolonged hunt for a giant coon, Tom became an easy mark for a stray hound that arrived at the Ferguson place one day.

"Named him Rover," said Tom. "Now there was a smart dog. He'd see me come out of the house with a shotgun and he'd start running rabbits. If I came out with a rifle he'd begin treeing squirrels. I'll tell you, that was the cleverest dog I ever saw.

"But I was determined to fool him," Tom continued. "Yes sir. So one day I left the shotgun and rifle in the house and came out carrying a fishing pole. Well, that dog took one look and began yelping and ran behind the barn.

"I couldn't imagine what had gotten into him," Tom said. "So I followed him to see what was going on. And there was Rover, behind the barn, digging fishing worms. I'll tell you I've never seen the equal of that dog."

# ROOSTER RIDGE

Well, shucks. Why look a gift chicken in the mouth.

Besides, as Bill Pitman argued, "I'm moving away and you need something running around up there anyway."

So Charlie and Lois Traveny took the chicken –er, that is – the chickens.

Trouble was, they came complete with roosters.

And the Travenys were not long in learning how that old man of song must have felt with a chick-chick here, there, and everywhere.

"They propagate," Charlie said and raised his eyebrows.

He was speaking of the many colorful bantams that roamed at will around the Traveny place.

They evidently did propagate. All over the hilltop.

A multiplication feat that moved Jim Jenkins to do something about it.

"He came over here one Sunday morning and said: 'Let's go set this tombstone.' and . . ." Charlie smiled. "You saw it on the way up." Charlie shook his head. "Jim's a friend of ours."

I did see the "tombstone" on the way up. It was at the foot of the hill right where the Traveny drive began, as a rectangle of gray limestone with rough-cut beveled edges. On the face of it was chiseled the following inscription:

CHARLIE-LOIS TRAVENY

in bold wavy letters, followed by three irregular lines of smaller letters which read:

Rooster Ridge
Where the cock-a-doodle doos
Do

"We can't stop them," Charlie smiled again. "We look for their nests but – have you ever tried to find a bantam hen's nest, or try to get to one after you do locate it?

"So we just let them have their fun. Pretty soon they'll come around parading a clutch of chicks behind. They really don't bother us," he said.

Under normal conditions Rooster Ridge was a din of strident bantam sounds. Roosters crowed hoarsely and constantly and hens clucked incessantly. Often the clucking had the quality of raucous urgency.

"One of them's laid an egg and three or four others have gathered around to congratulate her," Charlie said as he nodded at what sounded like a harsh dis-agreement among several of the dwarfed fowl.

The Travenys once attempted to reduce the number of bantams on their place by killing and dressing forty-four.

"But heck," Charlie again referred to their reproduc-tive exuberance. "They're back again."

The unlucky forty-four made good eating. Lois

warned that in preparing bantam roosters or hens for the dinner table her first mistake should be avoided.

"If you try to cook them as you do chicken you won't be able to stick a fork in the gravy, they're so tough," she cautioned. "You should fix them in a pressure cooker. Boiling is another way. They make good dumplings. And you can run the meat through a chopper and make chicken salad out of them. They're fine that way," she said.

We were seated in lawn chairs under a shade tree near the large white Traveny home high above Indian Creek. Brandy, a mixture of St. Bernard and collie, and Daisy, a basset, lay close, Hereford cattle chewed and swished in a nearby pasture, white geese and crested muscovy ducks waddled about on mysterious missions, and hummingbirds winged to and from a feeder at the house window and another at the barn.

"There are so many here in July and August that we have trouble counting them," Charlie said of the tiny birds. "I remember one time we thought there were a dozen at one feeder, then we decided there were fourteen. We changed our minds again and set the number at eight. But we really never did know, they move around so fast."

"They know when bad weather is coming," Lois picked up the narrative. "Just before a storm they'll come here in great numbers to fill up."

"Yes," her husband continued. "They'll perch on the light wires and on the awning cords to wait their turn."

Hummingbird feeding at Rooster Ridge began shortly after the Travenys arrived there more than nine years before my visit. In the beginning the tiny birds drank a pint of sugar-flavored water every four or five days.

"They came back each year with their young and now there are so many they eat one and one-half quarts a day. And it can get expensive," Charlie said, explaining that the mix was one cup of sugar to four cups of water. A cake coloring was used in the water so that the Travenys could determine at a glance its level in the feeders.

Charlie, a die-maker, was a native of Pennsylvania. Lois, a Hoosier, was from Salem. When they were house-hunting, the farmhouse and some forty acres on the Silverville-Armstrong Station Road was available. After seeing it their mutual opinion took the form of "Why not?"

During my visit they said things like "Living here is just great" and "There's nothing like it."

There were times, despite their joy, that, as Lois said, she would have liked to pick up the whole thing and moved it a mite closer to town.

"But," Charlie said, "we've learned that if you are going to need a fifty-cent item from the store tomorrow you pick it up on the way back from work today. From here it would cost two dollars to make a special trip into town."

Among the reasons for their attachment to Rooster Ridge was one that spoke warmly of the kind of neighbors the Travenys had.

"This is about as near as you will come to finding the old-time neighborhood you've heard so much about, where everybody helps everybody else," Lois began.

"They're something else," Charlie added. "If you need one of them, all you have to do is call. They'll come in a minute."

Before Bill Pitman moved away and left all his bantams with the Travenys the hilltop was called Traveny Terrace.

"After we got these chickens and roosters our friends constantly commented about them," Charlie said. "Since so many of them are roosters they find it hard to understand, and they ask us why. We tell them that with as many hens as we have here you have to have a lot of roosters to keep them all happy. They laugh. Then they comment on all the crowing and cackling that goes on here."

Of the many bantams that have lived on Rooster Ridge the Traveny's had made a pet of only one.

"The cow stepped on him," Charlie recalled. "We dressed and cooked him and we tried to eat him. But the more we chewed the bigger our mouthfuls got. We just couldn't do it."

# THE DANCE

These many years later I still smile wryly in the remembering. I do so now because of the date. What is sharpest in my reminiscing is a St. Patrick's Day vision of the diminutive Ruth Wrobeleska dancing on the bar at the neighborhood tavern.

I can also see Chuck, the bartender, black wavy hair, in starched white shirt and green bow tie, elbows spread like giant white wings, holding his head in both hands in mock horror.

And Frank, Ruth's husband, I can see him raise his glass of green beer and look over at me and wink. That's the way it was that night. Frank smiled a kind of sad smile and tipped his glass in silent resignation, or so I believed, to what was eating at his heart.

At that moment Ruth looked lovingly down at him, waved, threw back her head and laughed and waved to the applauding tavern patrons. Most of them wore green paper hats, tooted on green paper horns and whirled noisy green paper doo-dads.

In barrooms all over town, the faithful, along with a happy mixture of unbelievers, were paying homage to the patron saint of Bock Beer. Though the din discouraged normal conversation it did little to interfere with my thoughts. And while I watched her dancing in her stocking feet, up there on the bar, I remembered what little I knew about Ruth.

First of all I should clear up any misunderstanding. The kind of dancing Ruth was doing was not the heel-kicking, twirling, take-it-all-off kind you might expect in a booze joint.

Fully dressed in slacks and blouse, hands on hips, she moved slowly, smoothly, dreamily, turning now and then, and now and then waving to the revelers. Some of those might have thought it unusual that young Mrs. Wrobeleska, the neighborhood barber's wife, should be dancing in a barroom, and on the bar, of all places, but they knew nothing about Ruth.

By my standards even then Frank and Ruth were just a couple of kids, and both of them out of ethnic middle class families. I didn't know any of their people, but I learned a lot about them each time Frank put an apron around my shoulders and shaped a flat-top for which I had hair enough to wear in those days. And Frank told me about Ruth. After each session I thought I should write about her – them – but I couldn't. Tragedies have to take root in the soul, to season and to age there before the telling of them in print is possible.

That St. Patty's Day night I wondered how many of us knew that the seemingly happy, dancing Ruth was not long for this world. In the course of cutting hair Frank had surely confided this story to other of his customers. There was no way he could have kept it to himself. Telling it surely must have helped him retain his sanity and live with it.

Briefly, he and Ruth had grown up in the same neighborhood. They attended the same church, made their First Communion together, and went to the same parochial school and graduated together. Frank had never gone with another girl, and Ruth had never been alone with another boy.

From the very beginning they knew that they would some day marry and spend a lifetime together. But being who they were, children of Old World progenitors schooled in hardship and in homely virtue, they first had to obtain the permission of their parents. Anyone from that kind of background knows that takes time.

Frank went to barber school. For a few years afterward he worked in a shop downtown, saving to open his own neighborhood barber shop. When he was established, the interminable wait for old minds to reach new decisions was finally over. When she was nearer to thirty than twenty, Ruth's aged father gave her to Frank in a pretentious church ceremony.

A few months following the wedding, Frank came home after a long day at the barber shop to find Ruth unconscious on the kitchen floor. Although a city fire department rescue crew revived her on the way to the hospital, Ruth arrived in the emergency room a very sick still-new bride.

"It's in her lungs," a devastated Frank had confided while he was trimming my hair. "Both of them. It's unbelievable. She never smoked a cigarette in her life. Never took a drink. Always Cokes. It happened so fast."

The growth in Ruth's lungs might have happened as fast as Frank supposed. On the other hand it might have taken root years earlier and grown insidiously to lethal proportions. Doctors at the hospital couldn't be sure, Frank said. One thing they could be certain of was that Ruth didn't have a chance of beating it.

These were the thoughts that went through my mind that St. Patty's Day night. At the end of her dance some neighborhood guys who also got their hair cut at Frank's, and who also must have been aware of her illness, gently lifted Ruth down from the bar.

She laughed, happy with the applause her little show had evoked from the revelers, and took a sip from a glass of Coke. Frank introduced us and she thanked me for getting my hair cut in her husband's barber shop. Although she appeared tiny up there on the bar she seemed, if it was possible, much smaller standing between us.

"I just wanted to do it," she laughingly said of her spontaneous dance. "I thought it would be fun, and I just did it."

She continued laughing and her eyes were bright and her face was flushed with color.

The days of Lent passed that year and the week between Palm Sunday and Easter Sunday was a busy one for Frank. It seemed every man and boy in the neighborhood, and beyond, wanted to be neatly trimmed for Easter Sunday. Holy Saturday, the day before Easter, was exhausting for Frank; he had been busy cutting hair from morning until late night. He wasn't even able to take a lunch break.

Late getting home that night, weary and fatigued, he quietly  let himself into the darkened house. He looked forward to a relaxing hot shower that would help him sleep. Morning would come too soon, and there were church obligations. Earlier that week he'd had his suit dry cleaned and pressed and a white shirt laundered and starched. He would look his best for Easter Sunday.

In the darkness he carefully made his way to the living room and switched on a lamp. He saw his wife lying peacefully on the sofa. Deciding not to disturb her, he started for the bedroom to disrobe. Then changing his mind he quietly tip-toed to the sofa. Bending over his wife, in one swift motion, Frank carefully and gently kissed her on the lips. Ruth was as rigid and cold as marble.

# THE OLD DEPOT

I've sat in a few depots around the country in my time. New York. Philadelphia. Buffalo. Alberquerque. San Diego. Chicago. The floor of an abandoned rat-infested one even served as a welcome dry, but cold, bed for me one stormy night. But the one I enjoyed being in most of all was the old Monon Railroad depot at Owensburg.

There were no colorful milling throngs awaiting choo-chooing, shis-s-s-shing trains. There was no cry of "All aboard!" Nor was there the click-clack sound of a telegrapher's key. Still the charm of the place oozed memorably into the visit I had there with Cleve and Mary Smith.

"This was it," Mary gestured toward the bright comfortable room around us. "Our home was the Owensburg depot. And where we are now sitting was the waiting room."

"We gave ninety dollars for it and an acre and a half of ground," Cleve added. "That was in 1935. We were paying Bob Hudson a dollar and a half a month rent for a house in town and," he smiled wryly, "we had to find something cheaper."

Town was a quarter mile or more west of the depot

but the Smiths spoke of their home as being in Owensburg. It didn't look like a depot. Cleve explained that he had made several changes, including a front porch he built to replace what had served as the passenger platform for so many years.

The rails ran east from it to Bedford, and, as Cleve said pointing through a window, "west through that house over there," to Bloomfield. The agent's office and the telegrapher's key were in the center of the depot. The freight room was at the east end of the building.

"It was just a place to live when we came here," Mary remembered. "And we were as happy as if we had a fortune."

As we talked I was reminded that like a hidden tomb for a million memories the old railroad depot was still there. To find it one had to look under the renovations made with new siding, plaster, wallpaper, woodwork and carpeting. Cleve and Mary have long since been gone from there, but each time I view the house when I pass there on State Road 58 I remember my visit with them. "It was a sturdy building," Cleve informed me that day. "It was put up out of one tree – a big yellow poplar that came off the Moss place on Indian Creek. The framework and the siding are all one-by-twelve lumber."

He thought of something then that made him chuckle. "Living here made it easy for deliveries. When we'd have to have something sent out we'd say, 'Deliver it to the old Monon depot at Owensburg.' Everybody knew where that was."

"Our girls," Mary said of their two daughters Rhelda Horn and Janice Baker, "were never too pleased when we'd say things like that. It always embarrassed them to hear us say that we lived in the old Monon depot."

Mary's uncle, Charlie Miller, was one of the agents

at the depot during the active days of the railroad through Greene County. Tom Waggoner was another, as was Moses Cook. Remembering them Mary was reminded of the ticket window.

"I've wished a thousand times that we'd left the ticket window where it was in the middle of the room," she sighed. "It would have been a hole in the wall, I know, but," she laughed, "I could serve drinks through it."

One of the waiting room benches had been acquired and refinished by someone whose name was forgotten, and was on display in what then was Don and Patsy Foust's Gingerbread House Antiques in Owensburg. Something else in Gingerbread House, something that had brought me to Cleve and Mary's old depot home in the first place, was a replica of a child's folding rocking chair, as handmade as they come.

"My mother, Anna Strosnider, had this child's folding rocker when she was a girl," Mary began telling me the history of the chair. "After her death we found it in one of the outbuildings on her place. The cane seat was gone out of it, and there was some damage to the rest of the chair."

Cleve picked up the account from there: "We were sitting on the porch one day after I retired, and we got to talking about it. I decided to repair it. Before I finished I thought, 'Why not make one of these for each of the grandchildren.' I didn't think about what I was getting into," he smiled.

The couple had eight grandchildren and at the time of my visit with them Cleve had already furnished four of them with chairs. But the chairs became popular and he had made some thirty others. Three of them were in Colorado, one in Florida, one in Ohio, and one in Chicago. Another, completed shortly before my arrival, was destined for a home in California.

It was to fill in the idle hours of retirement that led Cleve to chair-making. That particular chair was chosen because it was Mary's mother's chair. Mary had played in it as a girl and Cleve and Mary's children had played in it.

"The kind of chair had nothing to do with it," Mary said of the uniqueness of that piece of furniture. "Nor did its age. It was where it had come from and where it had been that made it so valuable to us."

After the decision arrived at on the porch that day, Cleve built the first of his chairs from pieces of baseboard torn up from the interior of the old depot during its renovation. He later made them from native air-dried walnut, cherry, pine and poplar woods. At least one was made of redwood.

Cleve was at work in his shop one day when he accidentally jammed his hand into a routing plane. The wound required a half dozen stitches in his index finger and three more in his thumb to repair the damage. The mishap remained the talk of little Owensburg for a few days and just that quickly someone remembered Uncle Caswell Wilson.

No one ever called him Uncle Caswell, but just Uncle Cas. He was an aged Civil War vet who carpentered some but restricted his building to barns, and, like Cleve, to some smaller projects. Uncle Cas was first a farmer and then a carpenter. He lived on a farm near Owensburg and had several sons.

As Cleve had injured himself with a woodworking tool, so had Uncle Cas injured himself one day. Having contracted to build a barn for Matt Roberts, the old war vet hit his finger with a hammer. It was remembered by some folks in Owensburg who handed down the story as having been, "A pretty good lick because Uncle Cas cussed a blue streak."

Cussing being the best measurement of the degree of pain one suffers when striking a finger with a hammer, Uncle Cas could not have been expected to have done less than that. The greater the pain the more the cussing, the more intense the pain the louder the cussing. If you've ever hit your finger with a hammer you pretty well know all this, and how Uncle Cas must have suffered. To better understand, let me digress briefly.

As a youngster I was an altar boy and I knew a priest who when he hurt himself would say, "Oh sugar." No cussing for him, not a man properly ordained to the cloth. No cussing, that is, until one day while using a hammer and nails to repair a vestment drawer in the sacristy of the church he accidentally whacked his finger.

It too was a pretty good lick and it gave him much pain. He didn't say "Oh sugar," as usual. Not that time he didn't. The degree of pain he suffered was much greater than that. And while what he said could not in any way have been construed as being very sweet, it probably was the most honest measurement of pain ever to come out of his mouth.

Same with Uncle Cas. And, as the story goes, when he struck the same finger a second time he turned the air blue with the loudest cussing little Owensburg ever heard – and every cuss word right out of the book. There was no doubt in anyone's mind that Uncle Cas was really hurting.

That wasn't the end of it. Would you believe that the twice-hammered sore finger got in his way again that day and Uncle Cas struck it a third lick. But not a sound came out of the old soldier's mouth.

Oh, he got pale all right, and like gathered diamonds, beads of sweat suddenly sparkled his forehead. And his eyes popped out of their sockets almost to his cheekbones. But absolutely no sound came out of his mouth, not a single word, cuss or otherwise.

Matt, who was standing nearby and had heard the first two eruptions from Uncle Cas, could not believe what he was not hearing.

"How come you ain't cussin' this time like you did the first two times you hit your finger?" Matt asked, his curiosity finally overcoming him.

"Because," Uncle Cas replied as he slowly let the pressure off his clenched teeth, "I don't know enough cuss words to do this one justice."

Uncle Cas was a respected citizen and a beloved husband, father, and grandfather. The last was an attribute that followed him around as did his service to the Union. One day while he was stocking up on staples in the general store one of the town ladies mentioned how nice it was that a man would love his grandchildren as Uncle Cas loved his.

"Well," he replied, "grandkids are just fine, and I may be glad to see them come when they come. But," his voice seemed to take a little edge to it as he continued, "I'm always a hell of a lot gladder to see them leave when they leave."

Other than cussing so loudly when he whacked his finger with a hammer while building Matt's barn, Uncle Cas never created much of any other to-do around Owensburg unless, maybe, it was when he took a second wife.

"She was a fine lady, from Daviess County," the dimming memory was handed down by an Owensburg resident. "She had two grandchildren that she was raising, and they were also fine people. But they all were Catholics, the three of them, and we'd never seen any before. We didn't know what to expect. But she lived around here long enough with those two grand-children before Uncle Cas's death for us to find out Catholics didn't have horns."

Mary helped Cleve in his shop by doing the sanding, staining and varnishing of the folding rockers. One chair, Cleve revealed, required a net of five board feet. That reminded him that as a boy he had worked for his father Curtis Smith in the elder Smith's sawmill and almost any kind of lumber sold for a dollar a hundred feet, he said.

Cleve and Mary had been living in the old depot a number of years and already had their two daughters when Uncle Sam sent Cleve the dreaded "Greetings" that tore hundreds of thousands of Americans like him from their homes and families to serve in World War II.

"I was thirty years old when they drafted me," he remembered. "And right after basic training I was shipped out."

He served in New Guinea, the Philippines and Japan before he was to see Mary and the girls again. She remembered a strange letter she'd received from him during the war.

"He wrote and told me of this movie he'd seen about a ship being sunk, and about this guy saving himself and his buddy," she said.

A few days later the Army delivered to the old depot a telegram informing Mary that Cleve had been seriously injured at sea.

"The letter he wrote was about his own experience," said Mary. "It was the only way he could get it past the censors."

Cleve's ship, the LST *Ugly Duckling*, lead ship in a convoy of some thirty troopships headed for the Philippines, had taken two torpedoes in her side, breaking her in two.

"The break came right in the hold where I was sitting cross-legged on a lower bunk," Cleve recounted. "I had the good sense to grab a lifejacket on the way up from that hold, but I lost it."

After surfacing from the depths he found afloat a duffle bag and a folding cot which he used to support his weight in the water. Still later, from a makeshift raft, he swam, at the risk of his own life, to rescue a wounded buddy.

This latter part of his "experience" was related by Mary and she added that Cleve and his buddy, who then lived in Kentucky, still visited each other.

Cleve was eventually hospitalized in New Guinea. His records lost in the sinking of the *Ugly Duckling*, he had to re-join the Army there to be eligible for aid. Having also lost his shirt in the sinking of the LST, he had been denied mess privileges aboard a Navy hospital ship because of improper dress. After his release from the hospital his lack of GI clothing so angered an Army sergeant that Cleve was put on garbage detail.

"Everything was just about all right until then," he smiled ruefully at the memory, "Then that soured me on things."

To boot he was overlooked for a Purple Heart.

Cleve is gone now, and I suppose one Purple Heart or one letter of commendation, more or less, from the country he served, doesn't matter to him. But it seems to me that it ought to be noted in some conspicuous place or way that Cleve Smith, who lived with his wife, Mary, in a renovated railroad depot near the little town of Owensburg in Greene County, Indiana, once served his country with honor and distinction.

# CLEO

It is not surprising that when the hours got long and time got weighty that Cleo Willoughby should have wished to be back in the hardware store greeting old friends and making new ones.  She spent half her adult life there doing that.

Known as the Nashville Hardware Store, the establishment was situated on Jefferson St., just south of the old library building and across the street from the Methodist Church.  It was off the beaten path, meaning Van Buren St., the north-south main drag of Nashville.  But it was easily accessible, especially if one was aware that its rear door opened on an alley only steps away from the daily hustle and bustle of tourists.

Nashville Hardware Store included a small drygoods department on the north wall of the store which was visible from the outside through a large window on the west wall.  In earlier days that area housed a coin laundry.  When usage caught up with the appliances, and the washers and dryers began falling apart, Cleo decided to replace them with clothing and shoes.

"I sold a lot of little bib-overalls and a lot of shoes," she remembered during a visit at her home one day.

"A lot of bib-overalls for kids. I was famous for little overalls. People would say 'I want to buy the overalls that won't shrink for anything,' and that's what I used to sell them."

A mental picture of that end of the hardware store came to mind as we talked and I could again see the jeans and bib-overalls and western shirts, and shoes that she had displayed there. Nashville Hardware Store had been an occasional stop for me when my work took me to Tourist Town. Although it was easy to get to through an alley from Van Buren St., I always entered the store through the front door, like company. And each time I walked in I went directly to Cleo's husband, Gene Willoughby, who sat at the cash register, situated about the middle of the store, with his crutches propped nearby, and spoke a greeting.

We weren't friends, just acquaintances, but that's the way I handled my visits there. Sometimes I wondered if he remembered me from one visit to the next, so much time passed in between. But over the years I'd called often enough that he might have remembered me. At the risk of flattering myself, I think Cleo, although she was very quiet and reserved, remembered me. Gene and I would talk a while after which I'd take my leave. However, they were not warm, friendly talks, not like those he had with his friends.

"He had a lot of friends and they'd come in and loaf and talk till about eight o'clock at night," Cleo remembered.

I didn't have that kind of luxury, for I had other things to do. But we'd talk a while anyway. Cleo was always present, ever observant. She had come there from teaching school years before I became acquainted with the Willoughbys. After attending Indiana University she taught at Belmont, Green Valley, Pleasant Valley, Brown School on Salt Creek, and at

North Salem. At Belmont she taught four classes of twenty-eight kids in one room. At North Salem the picture was quite different: eight grades of forty-two boys and girls in one room.

Cleo remembered a near panic at North Salem when one of her charges, using an explosive powder, blew the seat off the pit toilet behind the school building. As is sometimes the case with teachers, she thought she knew immediately the identity of the culprit and she paddled his bottom. But her intuition proved faulty.

"I knew it was Rex Thompson Jr," she said. "But years later, long after I stopped teaching, he came into the store one day and he told me that I had got the wrong boy. He told me that he didn't do that."

So who did blow the seat off the outhouse at North Salem School? Unless someone confesses pretty soon, Cleo will never know, and neither will we. If it will help the culprit to come forward, Cleo said she was no longer angry about that little caper.

"I did get aggravated at my kids sometimes," she said of her teaching days. "But I loved them. And one of them, Rex Thompson Jr," she said, "still likes me," in spite of her mistakenly blaming him for rendering the outhouse useless at North Salem.

Cleo was a Kelley before she married Gene, and she came from a long line of school teachers. One was Eudora Kelley who lived on State Road 46 across from Kelley Gas Station at the top of Kelley Hill near the west gate of Brown County State Park. Mary Jane Kelley was another.

Leaving school one day Mary Jane made a fatal decision; she accepted a ride in a buggy with a friend. On the way home the horse bolted, the buggy upset, and Mary Jane was killed.

Cleo's uncle, Harry Kelley, also was a teacher. He also was operator of the gas station at the top of Kelley Hill.

Cleo said the house across the highway from the station was built by her great-great grandfather Benjamin Roten Kelley. That presumably was the origin of the name Kelley Hill.

Gene was a clerk in the hardware store when he and Bill Percifield decided to buy the place from Ralph and Mabel Burkholder. He later bought out Bill, and he and Cleo took it over. Gene spent a total of forty-four years there. Cleo figured she worked there thirty-five years.

On my visits to the store, Cleo was usually busy, busy, busy in her little corner, arranging and rear-ranging merchandise, dealing with customers or visiting with friends. It was memories such as those that kept coming back to her when the hours got long and time got weighty.

"I'd just love to be in the store," she revealed her fondest wish. "I'd love to see the people again. I enjoyed the store so much."

The store at this time was gone. Gene was gone. Many of her friends were gone. She had marked her eighty-sixth birthday a few days before my visit and, if she could have arranged it, she said she'd settle for a visit with those of her friends who remained, and be happy.

"I'd just love to see them," she said.

# LADY WONDER

Fascination with the unknown has been so great that numerous books on a variety of such subjects have provided their authors with many dollar comforts. One of these was the late Indiana newsman Frank Edwards.

Edwards compiled a series of writings on the unknown, including UFOs. But none of his researched articles equaled his own promotion of Lady Wonder, "the talking horse," while he was news editor of WTTV in Bloomington in 1955.

His version of the carnival affair surrounding that gifted equine appeared in an Ace Star Book entitled "Strangest Of All" which was authored by Edwards himself.

On the evening of Oct. 24, 1955 – an anniversary which few remember – listeners to Edwards' video news program heard him make a startling announcement. He had located a "talking horse" that held the secret to the whereabouts of a three-year-old Crane Village boy who had disappeared from his home earlier that month.

Ronnie Franklin Weitkamp at about 11:45 a.m. on Tuesday, Oct. 11, 1955, had walked away from his home and was never seen alive again.

The child's disappearance precipitated one of the most intensive searches in the history of Indiana. More than 2,500 sailors and marines barracked at the Crane Naval Ammunition Depot, and volunteers from all over the Hoosier state and from surrounding states, took part in the hunt for the missing child.

Unknown to them at the time, of course, was that little Ronnie must have died from exposure within twenty-four hours after he walked away from his home. His body was found almost two months later in a gully about a mile and a half from his door, over-looked by searchers who undoubtedly had walked within feet of him.

However, when the child was not immediately found, the possibility that he'd been kidnapped took root and began to grow. This certainly must have had a nega-tive effect on the overall efforts of searchers. Ronnie's photo appearing in newspapers and on television screens nationwide also held out the hope that he would be found somewhere other than near his home.

On a cold, rainy October night early in that search I sat in a tiny restaurant in the village of Scotland. Situated a few miles distant from Ronnie's home, it served as a rest stop for searchers. There I listened to the talk of weary men who, after braving a steady downpour and falling temperatures, were warming and fortifying themselves with food and hot drink. How far could a three year old walk, especially in the primitive terrain surrounding the Weitkamp home and Crane Village? Every foot, yes every inch of ground had been searched, it was believed. It was almost impossible that the child had been overlooked, even if he lay sleeping someplace, or dead.

If the little boy was not dead at that time his doom was shortly sealed by acts of good intent. Reports of a child fitting his description being seen with "a strange man" began coming in from all points. They were all false and misleading, and tended to disrupt the search. The publicity, as Edwards wrote, prompted a drunk in New Jersey to predict with almost psychic accuracy that little Ronnie would be found "buried in his own backyard."

The drunk's telepathic power, if that is what it was, fell only slightly short of that of Lady Wonder. The horse was introduced into the search for the child by Edwards' wife at breakfast on the 22nd of October, eleven days after the little boy's disappearance. Mrs. Edwards reminded her husband that Lady Wonder, who was stabled at Petersburg, Va., reportedly had given fantastic assistance to Massachusetts police in solving a crime. Why not call in the same equine brain about Ronnie's disappearance.

Why not? Edwards contacted "friends" in Washington, D.C., provided them with a list of questions, and asked them to visit Lady Wonder in her stall. The object of the visit was to get the necessary answers to Edwards' questions, obviously questions pertaining to Ronnie's disappearance.

As Edwards subsequently would explain to his growing viewing audience, Lady Wonder responded to questions by flipping up large tin letters which were suspended from a bar across her stall. Her owner charged fifty cents per question. At that time Lady Wonder was thirty years old.

As expected, the wise old horse came up with the desired answers to all the questions asked of her. Among them were questions about Ronnie Weitkamp, where he would be found, was he alive or dead, and when would he be found.

Lady Wonder, in her manner of speaking, said the

little boy would be found (she supposedly spelled out the words using the tin letters) in a "h-o-l-e near an e-l-m tree."

According to Edwards, when the animal was asked if Ronnie was alive, the horse further spelled out the word "d-e-a-d." When asked when his body would be found, Lady Wonder flipped three of the tin letters. First she flipped a "d". This was followed by an "e". And then a "c".

"Then," Edwards reported, "she turned and shuffled out of the stable," ending the interview with his name-less friends from Washington, D.C.

On the following Sunday, Dec. 4, "two teen-age boys," Edwards later recounted, found the remains of Ronnie Weitkamp in a gully about a mile and a half from his home. The nearest tree was an elm.

Actually there were three boys who made the dis-covery: John Medina, Jim Gentry and Willard Neyhaus as reported in the media.

Lady Wonder had informed her questioners that Ronnie would be found within a mile of his home. She was wrong by half a mile. The drunk in New Jersey was wrong by a mile and a half.

# "MY BRIDGE"

They had names of their own and were as individual as you and I. The Bell, for example, and the Nancy Jane. They were a necessity in their time, but their need extended deeper into the human soul than few today can imagine.

They were rural halls of fellowship, shade from the summer's sun, shelter from sudden rains, and lazy places in which to sit and talk.

Their greatest following came from the ranks of the rural young, and it was inside them that the crude artistry of the pocketknife flourished.

It was also, within their darkened interiors that hands touched secretly, and lips dared to kiss.

The Bell, the Nancy Jane, the Goodman, the Fairfax, and so many like them, gone. And as of the night of June 20, 1976, the last of them, the Williams Covered Bridge across Bean Blossom Creek about five miles northwest of Bloomington, disappeared from the Monroe County landscape.

First believed to have been struck by lightning, it was later suggested that the old bridge may have been the victim of arson. About a hundred and twenty-five feet long, the span had collapsed into the creek bottom.

"It was lost before we could get there," said Larry Stanger, chief of the Bloomington Township Fire Department, and for whose grandfather the bridge was named.

Like its predecessors, the Williams, believed to have been ninety-seven years old, had known many human attachments. One of its fondest, perhaps, was that of a small boy taking a whole day to carve his first and last names across its wooden ceiling with his pocketknife, while a sweet girl watched.

The bridge got its name from its location, on the Happy Williams farm. It had been known by other names during its long life – McMillan, Milligan and Mulligan – but the name Williams endured.

As lasting as that name was, the name given it by a gracious, elegant lady whose father helped build the bridge also endured. She had grown up on a hillside from which she could look down on it. And she lived near it all her life.

"I called it 'My Bridge,'" said Ruby Williams while wisps of smoke still rose from the charred and broken skeleton of the bridge that lay in the creek bottom.

"I remember it all my life," she said. "Way, way back. Ever since I can remember. And when my husband was a boy he and his friends used to gather in the bridge. His initials were WWW, which he could carve quite well, and he carved them all over the inside, and I admired them every time I went through it."

Before she married Wayne W. Williams, son of Happy Williams, she was Ruby McNeely, daughter of M.C. McNeely. Her father used to operate a grocery store on the hill above the bridge. Twice each week he traveled over it to Ellettsville to pick up mail for farmers in the surrounding countryside.

When the government learned of this, McNeely was asked to identify his "post office." And he did so by taking the name of a city in California from which he'd recently received a letter from a relative – Modesto.

There was never a town there, but McNeely's store served a large community, as did the Modesto Post Office.

Early in 1966 Bloomington Mayor John H. Hooker, Jr. favored removing the Williams Covered Bridge from Bean Blossom Creek to Griffy Lake, where it could be preserved as part of Monroe County's past.

Monroe County Commissioners also saw the wisdom in that plan. But there was opposition to reconstructing the bridge anyplace else, and the project was abandoned.

Two years later the bridge underwent repairs, and again in 1970 it was repaired. Some twenty thousand dollars was spent on it in the latter year, replacing an old shingle roof with metal, and adding steel supports to the bridge.

In 1974 someone drove an old car into the bridge and set it ablaze, but the span was saved. In previous years the Bell Bridge on Kinser Pike was burned. The Gosport Covered Bridge across White River was also burned, and a volunteer fireman lost his life in that blaze.

On the night of June 20 that same weird fate struck the Williams.

At her home, where for a good part of her life she could hear each passing car and truck rattle the bridge's floorboards, Ruby Williams revealed her emotions after learning the bridge had burned while she slept that night.

"I felt let down," she said. "I felt very sad. I could have cried, but I didn't."

**The Williams Bridge**
(Monroe County)

The emotional impact was slow in coming to many Monroe Countians. First reports identified the bridge correctly as the Williams Covered Bridge. And most of those who heard believed the tragedy had struck the covered bridge that spans the East Fork of White River at Williams, Ind.

Ray Cavanaugh once wrote in verse that covered bridges are a "symbol of ways no longer with us."

Monroe County now lacks both the ways and the symbol.

In his ode to the bypassed covered bridge at Medora, in Jackson County, Clyde Lingle Gilbert was inspired to refer to the span as a landmark of rare beauty, having carried man, wagon and steed. The sentiment, the last verse of which appears below, seems a fitting tribute to the Williams Bridge.

*Farewell covered bridge, it's like losing a friend.*
*Thousands will miss you on to the end.*
*You've done a good job by serving us well,*
*Leaving true reminiscences for history to tell.*

# NICKEL-BACK

It was sometime after midnight. A half-block from the Bedford public square an automobile moved stealthily west in the alley between 14th and 15th streets. A noisy freight train pulled by a chugging steam locomotive thundered along J Street.

At the head of the alley an object thrown from the car shattered a window in a small building there. The automobile turned onto J Street and, moving parallel to the train, raced away. Muffled by the rumbling freight, few if any people in town heard the explosion that followed.

The small building was blown into kindling. Downtown J Street in that vicinity was a rough and tough place. In that block alone there were a tavern, a liquor store, at least one pool room, and three small hotels that served the needs of an assortment of the town's sporting ladies. A decent woman, as one old timer remembered, wouldn't walk there in those days.

But the street's dubious reputation had nothing to do with the bombing. On the contrary, it was a harmless barber shop that was blown up. Trouble was there were too many of them in town, thirty-six, to be exact, and that particular one had become far too popular.

"It was a price war, and it got serious," barber Dale Marley remembered. He had paused with shears and comb upraised while an apron-covered client and I listened in his single-chair shop one day. "It was my dad's shop. Jess Marley was his name. He and my two brothers Jim and Bill, and Clarence Mosier, cut hair there.

"Nickel-back, people used to say of it," he said. "Haircuts were fifteen cents and shaves a dime. When kids got a haircut my dad would give them back a nickel. People used to say to young prospective haircut customers, 'Hey, want a nickel back? Go to Marley's.' They cut more hair in my dad's shop than all the rest of the shops in town. Barbers were losing their homes because they weren't making enough money to pay the mortgage. That's why they bombed the place."

Jess Marley wasted no time. Obtaining a piece of ground across J Street from his former shop, he built a five-chair shop there between the tavern and one of the popular hotels, and his success continued. Jess Marley eventually moved on to partake of his promised reward. The tavern, its devotees, the hotels and their hard working ladies, the pool room, all are gone too. With the passing of more time, that once exciting block of J Street became all but deserted and somnolent. But Dale Marley, who started shining shoes at age ten, and cutting hair at age twelve under his father's tutelage, remained in the same shop – still a busy, wide-awake place – long enough to share this memoir.

"My father was the best damn barber to ever hit this town," he remembered fondly. "He was just

106

about cut in two by a machine gunner in Germany in World War I. And he was getting a hundred percent disability. He shouldn't have been working. But he was a worker. He'd cut hair all day here in the shop. Then he'd go home to Trinity Springs and cut hair half the night with a hand clipper under kerosene lamps and a Coleman lantern hanging over the chair. We used the same Coleman lantern to go fish-gigging and coon hunting. My dad was the best man I ever knew, the best friend I ever had.

"Kids wouldn't get their hair cut any place else," Marley talked on. "They wanted that nickel back, you see. Dad was good to people, too. He would give unemployed people money to buy groceries in those Depression days, too, and never say anything about paying it back. But he would say, 'Remember where to get a haircut when you find a job.'"

By this time a second client, Lowell Smith, had ascended Marley's workplace. The son of Bedford inventor Otho Smith, he also shared some memories of his father. He was followed by nonagenarian Raymond Stultz, of whose full head of white hair Marley said without exaggeration "is the prettiest you'll ever see," and who, Marley said, was retired from the Bedford post office.

Stultz's presence reminded Marley of an early desire. "I didn't want to be a barber," he said with a shake of his head. "I wanted to work for the post office, to be a mailman. I just wanted to walk up and down the street delivering mail. But my dad wanted me to be a barber."

Remembering an early J Street dweller Marley said that with a jug of whiskey in one arm and a sporting lady on the other the guy would party so long in one of the hotels across J Street, "When he came out he looked like a groundhog. And he'd stop in here for me to shave him."

Marley didn't hesitate to remind me that the front door of the old *Times-Mail* newspaper, standard bearer of Bedford's early moral majority, opened on J Street only a few steps away from the action. The paper made no crusading efforts to clean up the place.

"It's an experience to come in here," Smith, with a big smile, had earlier spoken the understatement of my visit with Marley.

Marley smiled too. "I grew up barbering on this street ever since I was twelve years old," he said. "I never went to college but I'll guarantee you I've gotten an education."

A personable, friendly man who in earlier years had caught the interest and attention of other newspapermen, and had his name and picture in the paper, Marley nodded his head. And he added, "Dad once said to me, 'If you didn't talk so damn much you could cut twice as much hair. You talk so much you ought to be a preacher.'

"Well, I can do that too," he smilingly admitted as he slipped into a sobering evangelical message. "You see," he advised at its finish, "if a barber wants to keep his customers he has to be an entertainer too. Some people don't have the personality to be a preacher or a barber. If you ain't got it, you won't be a success at either one."

At sixty-six, Marley counted his barber shop years back to 1940, and his friends by the score. He had never taken a vacation. Married to Kathryn Parker, they lived in Bedford and were the parents of a son and daughter.

"She is the greatest woman who ever lived," Marley said proudly of his wife.

They had a black, thirteen year old Lab-Irish Setter mix named "Skeeter," whom he said had "big white teeth this long –" he held up the length of the barber shears "– that will bite your arm off. He's the greatest dog that ever lived," he gave a convincing downward movement of his chin. "And he is crazy about country western music."

Marley remembered that the late Bedford attorney Bob Mellen, highly respected and successful in his field, once told him, "Marley, you could out-talk a radio."

To which the esteemed Marley acquiesced with grace and nobility.

# MATTIE FAUBION

Mattie Faubion may have had good cause to believe she'd been "just about through the book," as she insisted while reviewing her ninety-three years. But my visit with her at her Heltonville home indicated something more than that – a spirit as welcoming as the first fragrance of wild roses in June.

She was a small woman, slight in stature and frail as a sparrow. Yet her conversation moved with the alacrity of one always on the threshold of new adventure. But because her physical strength often failed her, especially when she was in the notion of mopping her kitchen floor, Mattie was resigned to giving up and finding a place to sit. In exasperation she would declare at those times, "If the Lord is ready for me, I'm ready to go."

When given the advantage of occasional spurts of physical strength, however, Mattie was quick to say, "I don't want to go yet. Not when I can do the things I want to do."

Those things, in addition to mopping the kitchen floor, included attending church services, visiting with friends, cutting rug rags, piecing quilts, and making weekly visits to the senior citizens center.

"I'm the oldest member there," she would say proudly. And like as not she would add, "I'm the oldest member wherever I go."

Mattie grew up in the *redbrush*, a sassafras patch she would pinpoint in the following manner: "You go up to the railroad tracks, turn left, and go a couple of miles. And that's it."

She said she was left alone there at a tender age, was allowed only to attain the second grade at the one-room Fullen School, and paid for her keep by working in a boarding house owned by a relative. When we met she was one of a diminishing number of people who remembered the Heltonville of old, and when she spoke of it she attached to her recollections the names of businesses there.

"Jep Newkirk sold coffins," she remembered a few for my sake. "Scott Clampitt had the saloon. Elmer Ramsey had the drug store, and he sold whiskey there. And George Ross had the shoe shop."

Mattie was aware that because of her lack of schooling she had missed some of life's pleasures. Her disappointment was revealed when she spoke of her inability to read what she called "big words."

That she might have taken much from more years in school was evident from her memory of that second grade and the lessons taught her. She recalled a reading lesson and recited it for me as she once did for her teacher at Fullen School.

"Two little kittens one stormy night," she began, "began to quarrel and then to fight. One had a mouse, the other had none, and that's the way it begun.

"'I'll have that mouse,' said the little one. 'No you won't,' said the big one. The old woman took her sweeping broom and swept both kittens out of the room.

"The ground was covered with ice and snow, and the

two little kittens had nowhere to go. They lay on the mat at the door while the old woman was sweeping the floor. Then they crept in as quiet as mice, and found it was better, on a stormy night, to lie by the fire than to quarrel and fight."

She did not hesitate when I asked for an encore, and she again recited from memory:

"The old hen she laid her laying out, and she was going to hatch some little chicks. The old rooster came up and said, 'Will you take a walk with me, my little wife, today? There's barley in the barley fields and hayseed in the hay fields.'

"'No,' said the hen. 'My chicks will soon be hatched, and I'll think about it then.'

"'Crack! Crack!' went the eggs, and out came the chicks small. 'Cluck!' said the clucking hen. 'Now I have you all. Come along my little chicks, I'll take a walk with you.'

"'Hello,' said the rooster proud. 'Cocky-doodle-do. I guess I'll go too.'

"And they all went down the lane together."

Mattie had ten little chicks of her own. The youngest at this time was fifty years old.

"They're still your *children* no matter how old they get," she told me.

Mattie lived by a simple philosophy. "You've got to love everybody, and you can't hold a grudge," she put it simply. "You might as well be mad as hold a grudge."

In all her years she had never smoked, never consumed an alcoholic drink, and had never danced. But she said she knew of many women in her time who did all three, and more.

"I lit many an old woman's pipe with a hot coal," she said. "They kept a fire going outside all the time, and when someone wanted to light a pipe you'd put a hot coal on the tobacco in it for them. Fanny Thomas smoked a pipe, and I can still see her putting a rusty finger down on that hot coal. Women chewed plug tobacco, too. One would sit in her door and so that passersby wouldn't see the evidence, when she'd have to spit she'd turn and spit in her door, instead of outside."

Toward the end of my visit I prepared my camera to make a photograph of Mattie. When she saw what I was doing she gasped, "Oh for John's sake, are you going to take my picture?"

Receiving an affirmative reply, she said, "Well, wait until I pull my socks up and blow my nose."

# THE PROUD FIREMAN

It was January, 1937. Four new appointees to the Bloomington Fire Department reported for duty: Hollis "Ditty" Van Dyke, Harry McNeeley, Noble Henderson and Bernard Glover.

Cotton Brandt was mayor. Loba "Jack" Bruner was sheriff. Bert Hazel was fire chief. A probationary fireman's pay was twenty-four dollars a week. Good money? To a good man with four children, like Glover, *big* money.

Try these names to quicken recollection, or to stir your curiosity: Leon Dillman, Horace Robertson, Rollie Crum, Ray Collier, Paul Lentz, Carl Hawkins, Millard Axsom, Fred Koontz, Roger Coan, John Thrasher, Silas Crum, Willis Lawhead, Clarence Brewer, Arthur Retzlaff, Jewitt Wampler.

All Bloomington firemen of that distant time.

Not from my memory.

Glover's.

Also from his memory of that time: a "new" Ford fire truck, an Ahrens-Fox, and a Stutz; the city's total collection of fire-fighting equipment that greeted him and the other new men. All housed at what then was Central Station, at Fourth and Walnut.

Some reminiscences he shared included the Harris Grand Theater fire. "It had such a terrific start," he remembered. "A theater is like a church, all that air space. And we just lost it. And that was with a lot of citizen help."

He recalled the Greyhound bus disaster, too, in which he said eighteen persons perished on the night of August 10, 1949. Eighteen people killed in placid, rural Monroe County, west of Dolan on Old State Road 37. In the ensuing years it became Old Old State Road 37, or the Old Martinsville Road. There were no township fire departments at that time.

Glover recalled for me:

"The bus hit a bridge abutment. I rode the rig that night. Jewitt Wampler drove. When we got there people were in the bus, sitting like statues. Dead. Burned to death. There had been some terrible screaming. Then silence. We had a second truck there in a matter of minutes. We put the fire down so they could get the bodies out. We've had some bad fires. Nothing like that one. It kind of put you in a daze."

He recalled another:

A mother and two small children in a trailer fire. Carelessness. Stuff stored around the back door. A virtual barricade. People will do that. They also have been known to remove the knobs off mobile home back doors to keep little children from falling or straying outside.

A warning from the past still good enough for today:

"People get careless about the simplest things," the old fireman said.

He was up in years at this time. Seventy-six. And proud. A native of Solsberry who came to Bloomington as a boy, he left a laudable heritage. He'd served twenty-seven years on the department, and six more years in the State Fire Marshal's office. Along the way he helped rear four children.

"I took an interest in the total fire service from the beginning," he told me. "I was interested in better working conditions for firemen all over the state, better wages, better equipment and more men."

Glover's star began its ascent on another January day in 1939. Democrat Bruner took over the reins of the city and appointed him chief. He was also chief during the mayoral terms of Tom Lemon and Mary Alice Dunlap.

"It makes a man extremely proud," he said of having served with distinction all those years.

He added these words to remember and to apply to our own lives:

"The life of a fireman is hard, but it has its rewards. I was always proud to be a fireman, and I was proud of my work. If a man is a good fireman he must get a good feeling out of the work he does."

The four Glover children included Robert, Richard, Gordon and Philip (Bud). Gordon followed in his father's footsteps and served twenty years as a Bloomington fireman. The other person who helped rear them, the woman who lovingly and faithfully stood by all of them, father and sons, was Maude Williams Glover. They were married in 1920. At the time of her death they had been together fifty-six years.

My call at his kitchen door shortly after her passing was a surprise. He was engaged in sorting the things of their long life as husband and wife, father and mother, friends, trying to decide what should be saved, what should be given away.

It happens, you know. And like anyone else, he was having a difficult time of it.

Rather than being an interruption, my visit, he

**Bernard Glover**

said, was a break for him, one he appreciated. But the chore did not go away; it would await him till I left. Death had taken away a wife, a mother, and grandmother. It was not easy. It would not be easy. Their eventual separation by death was not unexpected. Yet, as reflected in his daily prayer, the life of a fireman does not prepare him for such a sequence. As I remember, these are some of the words of the prayer he spoke to me:

". . . and if I am to lose my life, please bless with Your protecting hand my children and my wife."

Nothing about the departure of a wife, for women are supposed to outlive their men. The prayer contained no requests for instructions for an old fireman left behind.

*In his book "Relive it . . . with C. Earl East," (Copyright 1963 by C. Earl East, Bloomington, Ind., Inter-Collegiate Press, Inc.) the author notes that sixteen persons burned to death when a Greyhound Bus struck a bridge abutment north of Bloomington.*

*Fifteen of the passengers were trapped inside the bus when it overturned. Almost instantly flames burst up from the floor and they perished immediately.*

*Twelve persons escaped the flames with various injuries and burns and one of them died later at Bloomington Hospital.*

# THE MUSICIANS

Ellen Wright smiled as she opened with a flurry the sheet music on the piano in front of her.

"This is just a little rag piece," she said, "that somebody brought in here one day. 'Skeleton Rag.' I thought it was pretty cute."

Within seconds syncopated rag tones filled the music room of the tall, two-story, twelve-room house and tumbled tunefully and rhythmically out the screen doors and windows into the streets of Tunnelton where they shamelessly shimmered and shook in the oppressive heat of late June.

When they at last came to a halt Aunt Ellie – she was Aunt Ellie to all who knew her – closed an eye in what appeared to be the equivalent of a wink, and smiled again.

"I've been trying to play the piano ever since I was born," she said in mock disappointment.

Considering the amount of time that had lapsed between then and the day she played the ragtime piece for me, not to mention a lively rendition of "Stand Up, Stand Up For Jesus," her effort had certainly begun to pay off. So much so that in the ninety-four years since her birth numerous young people had allowed her to teach them as much as she could of what she had learned.

"Terri McCart," she began naming a few of the students who weekly joined her for instructions in the two-piano music room. "Terri plays at the Methodist Church, here in Tunnelton. And Paula Dorsett. She plays at that Methodist Church in Lawrenceport. And Susan and Kim Weaver. They play at the Methodist Church in Bono. I'm teaching them to play in Sunday School, but they play for the church services sometimes."

They represented the last of innumerable students she had taught.

"I can't even begin to remember their names," she said of the others. "Sometimes one will come up to me and say, 'I took from you,' and then he'll have to tell me who he is."

Aunt Ellie began her teaching career immediately after completing her studies at the Indianapolis Conservatory of Music. In addition to those students whom she taught in the music room where she had played the ragtime piece for me, she had also instructed several students in Medora and Vallonia.

"I used to take the B&O train right here in Tunnelton and go to Vallonia," she recalled those early days. "I'd teach all day there and then come back this way to Medora, where I'd stay the night. I'd teach there the next day and then come back to Tunnelton on the train that evening."

One such trip was interrupted by the devastating flood of 1913.

"My brother got so worried about me he left here in a buggy to look for me," she recalled. "He found a way on the high ground to get to Medora. When they told me he was there I got out of an upstairs window into a boat. I'll tell you," she paused to laugh at the memory, "that was something."

Once in the boat they ran into problems, Aunt Ellie remembered.

"We didn't get very far when the boat got caught on the top of a fence post, and we just sat there going around and around, like that," and she made circles with a long, thin hand. "I'll never forget that," she said breathlessly.

The pianos in the music room at Aunt Ellie's were a Hardman Cabinet Grand, which bore the date 1842, and a Packard upright.

"I practice techniques every day," she said of her continued teaching and ability to play. "I have arthritis so bad in these fingers," she held up a hand, "that it is hard to do. But I practice one to two hours every day. It keeps these fingers limber."

One day when Aunt Ellie began playing on the keyboard of the Packard upright, her neighbor across the street complained that she was making a lot of unnecessary noise.

"I just shut the door," Aunt Ellie made a stern face, "and I went on playing. Now he just sits there and listens to me."

That was the only complaint she had ever had. People generally enjoyed hearing her play. She had rattled piano keys for numerous shindigs with fiddler John R. Smith, a nearby Tunnelton resident. She was also church pianist for many years.

"I just love to play the piano," she said.

She offered some advice to piano teachers. "A half hour," she said of short lesson periods, "is not long enough. It takes an hour to teach a good lesson." And to piano students she admonished, "Practice, practice, practice. Two hours a day, at least."

Thirteen years before I visited with her, Aunt Ellie fell and fractured a hip. At worst the mishap barely slowed her down. She continued playing the piano at church, making her way on a walker. She was still using a walker around the house. But when she chose to ignore it she substituted chair backs, tables, even the pianos.

The large home that surrounded her was almost as charming as Aunt Ellie. Tall, white, boxlike, with a black iron fence, it was an elegance of aging high ceilings, high, inside-shuttered windows, and beautifully scrolled door and window casings. East Lawrence Water Corporation water was piped into the house but Aunt Ellie preferred well water from a pump mounted on the kitchen sink drainboard.

On this, the occasion of her ninety-fourth birthday, she happily served cake and ice cream to those of us who were gathered there. And she announced with a melodic chortle that she not only had never been married, but that, "It doesn't look like I ever will be."

Remembering her Aunt Ellen Wilcox, who knew an exceptional longevity and required in her old age all the care Aunt Ellie could give her when she wasn't teaching the piano, her tone changed.

"You see," she said in a serious vein, "I was pretty busy right here, and I didn't have time to think about marrying."

But she did not tarry over the past. Mercy! Well-wishers had twice brought in cake and ice cream. Who wanted to be blue on a happy birthday?

Aunt Ellie once said of John R. Smith that if she hadn't heard him play the piano in fifty years she would recognize him and his style of playing if she were blindfolded.

That's what John R. remarked as he paused with

his large hands over the keyboard of the old Holland player piano which was manufactured in Minneapolis and which was in his home.

"I've been told the same thing in a derogatory manner, too," he smiled good naturedly as his hands fell to the keyboard where they syncopated "Meet Me In Dreamland Tonight."

Sitting sidesaddle on the arm of an overstuffed chair near the piano, I listened fascinated while John R. moved right into "Shine On Harvest Moon" with those big fingers of his delicately touching the white and black keys.

"There've been a lot of legs broken dancing to that one," he looked up at me. "It is one of the grandest songs that ever was written."

When you listened to John R. syncopating on the piano you envisioned things like the clear rippling Leatherwood Creek at Otis Park in Bedford on a bright day, or the old red and rusted iron bridge over quiet, green Guthrie Creek, or the lowlands far below the Devil's Backbone, and the easy curves of Goosecreek Road in the shadow of the hills to the southwest.

John R. and his wife, Mabel, had shut down all but two rooms of their Tunnelton house for the winter. People used to do that. It was less strain on a woodchopper's back, for one thing, and, for another, it made for a cozier winter. Mabel had also shut down the Tunnelton General Store. She had renewed her retail license but the store was finished. A thing of the past.

"I'm syncopating all these old songs, even the waltzes," John R. said. It didn't matter that I didn't quite understand the term "syncopating." I was used to playing a typewriter, not a piano. And he went on to further enhance my knowledge of the piano by playing a "double triplet," which Aunt Ellie avowed just couldn't be done.

"'But John R. does it,'" he mimicked her as she was quoted to him by someone else.

At this time John R. had attained his three score and ten, plus one. At the piano he was at least half that age, maybe younger. If you could have listened to him play and sing the lyrics to "Telephone," you'd have probably said, "eighteen!" And he would have backed your impression, as he did mine, with "Hello my baby, hello my honey, hello my ragtime gal; send me a kiss by wire, honey my heart's on fire . . ."

The two shut-off rooms became cozier by the second as John R. played and sang.

"That song came out when the telephone came into use," he explained when he reached its last notes. And then he was off and into other oldies, including, "Morning Prayer."

When he was six years old John R. was given a five dollar fiddle for Christmas from his dad, a two-dollar and fifty cent case in which to store and carry it, and a bow.

"He bought it in a drug store in Mitchell," John R. recalled. "And when he got home he strung that fiddle up and showed me how to play 'Old Dan Tucker' before he and my older brother went out to the barn to do the evening chores. Well, I suppose it took about an hour to do them chores and when they got back I could play that song."

After a moment's pause he smiled, "I was smarter then. It takes me a little longer to learn a song now."

He did an about face on the piano bench and reached for one of several fiddles lying around on tables in the room just as Mabel said, "Play 'Snow Deer.'" And to me she said, "That one goes back 'fore we was ever married."

In John R.'s big hands and against his thick six-foot body the fiddle looked like a toy. But that didn't keep him from making some foot-stomping music come out of it. He then did the same with another fiddle, and another, and another – fiddles he himself had made – crafted – over the years. And he talked about each one as though it were a child, recounting its birth and development and its idiosyncrasies.

He'd caress a fiddle and say, for example, "I feel fiddle-making reached its perfection in the 1700s. But you still try to achieve a charm in the tone of one that no other one has."

This man who had a copy of every book that Harold Bell Wright had published, a copy of most of Zane Grey's, simply inundated me with his piano playing and his fiddling and his knowledge of music. I sat there in awe of him as he switched from piano to fiddle and back with renditions of "Red Wing," "By The Light Of The Silvery Moon," "Under The Double Eagle," and so many more, more, more, including "The Old Soft Shoe." And I wondered where he found the time to read. It was all so very, very wonderful.

"That's something no violin-maker ever tells," he informed me after I had asked him how many fiddles he had crafted in his lifetime. "Why, that's the worst bad luck in the world, to tell how many you've made. But you can say I've made maybe – maybe," he put strong emphasis on the word, "– one a year for the last fifty years."

Being one of those people with an insatiable curiosity I wondered where they were, who had them, and did they know as much as I about the man who made them. Fearing John R. might construe further questions on that subject as an attempt on my part to determine the number of fiddles he had made, and bring him bad luck, I refrained from asking him more.

John R. wrote music for piano and violin and, although he said he knew music, he wanted me to know that he played by ear. Here's the way he explained that: Say he heard a song and wanted to play it. He would learn the tune – now this is what he meant by playing by ear – then write the music for it, as he had heard it, then he learned to play it. Afterward he no longer needed the music, he said.

That probably was only one of his musical talents that prompted Aunt Ellie to say that if she had not heard him play in fifty years she could tell it was John R. if she was blindfolded.

John R. believed that since violin-making had reached the epitome of craftsmanship in the 1700s, the fine instruments being made in our time would come into their own in fifty years.

"It's the aging of a finely made instrument that can't be duplicated in the making of it that makes its every note a beautiful chord," he said. "We needn't worry. We know how the old masters made them, and we will continue to have fine instruments."

# THE OLD MAN

His jaw pushed outward, his chin rose, his lips pooched and flapped. Each time he made the sounds I could not hear, his head tilted back, like a dog will do when it barks.

Because I was passing in a car I was unable to hear him. But after applying my skills at lip reading, and seeing a barking dog nearby, I was willing to wager that he was barking at the dog. An old man barking at a dog.

If he was not barking at a dog then he was sucking air in a very strange manner. But he and the dog seemed to be exchanging words.

At the next corner a churchyard parking lot offered a stopping place. I got out of my car there and waited for him. As I watched him approach he moved slowly. Shuffling in the manner of the elderly, feet in the comfort of shiny, brown lounging slippers, he came. I noticed that the slippers had sturdy heels and high tops with elastic side panels, the kind elderly men wear.

Slight of stature, he moved totteringly, precariously, his small arms bent at the elbows, gnarled hands held in front of him, miming the stance of the late actor James Cagney. The cuffs of his stove-pipe black pants hung wrinkled on the glistening tops of the lounging slippers. The white shirt he wore was white-white and nicely pressed, the collar open.

A golfer's hat, the brim snapped down in front, the single visible vestige of his younger days, was tipped dinkily forward on his small head. Fragile frameless glasses perched on his nose took up much of his tiny face. When he was close enough I was aware of the refreshing fragrance of soap, maybe shaving cream, for he was pink and white clean, and smooth shaven.

"You don't know me –," I started to introduce myself. I was taking a negative approach as I usually did when dubious circumstances left me unsure of myself. I was hoping to come up with an anecdote for my newspaper column, but it looked as though I wasn't going to have any luck.

"Already know that," he interrupted me with a voice that sounded as frail as he looked. He was near enough that his blue eyes shone bright and clear behind clean lenses.

"I'm sorry." I took another tack. "I was driving by and I thought I saw you barking at a dog back there."

"Was," he said tersely.

"Why?" I asked quickly, afraid that given time to think he might decide to ignore me and walk on.

"He barked at me." The statement sounded almost like a challenge. To myself I thought, can I possibly write about this? Then I spoke to him again.

"Why did you bark at him, really?"

"Shuts him up."

The old gentleman was not wasting words.

"How does that shut him up?"

"Ask him," the man snapped, jerking a thumb in the direction from which he had come.

"He did shut up, then," I queried, noting the paleness of his thumb, and that the dog was still barking back there.

"Every time," he replied.

I was honestly curious and he had left me an opening to pursue my questioning.

"You've barked at him before?"

"Every day that it ain't raining."

"You mean – ?"

"Every day that it ain't raining I walk along this sidewalk. Every time I walk here that animal tears out and barks at me. Makes a terrible racket."

The long answer left him puffing for air for a few moments.

"Every time," he repeated.

"Do other people ever wonder why you bark at him?"

"They never asked me," he growled.

I thought the man sounded angry, at least annoyed, with me.

"I'm sorry. I didn't mean to offend you."

"You haven't," he snapped.

"That dog," I nodded in the direction from which he'd come. "Do you know him – I mean – do you know his father and moth –" I tried rescuing myself, "I mean do you know his –"

The old man was staring at me in such a way that I could not continue making the correction. I felt incredibly stupid and uncomfortable.

"Who are you?" he asked, frowning in my direction.

I pronounced my first and last names, the last slowly, clearly. The old man shook his head.

"What kind of a name is that?"

"The last one? Oh, that one is Italian," I said. "But what I really wanted to say was do you know the folks who own that dog?"

"Eye-tal-yan?"

He was peering at me as though he might have been looking for distinguishing features that might set me apart from the human race. I gave him enough time for a good look and to make up his mind before answering him.

"Yes." I finally said.

"Eye-tal-yan, eh?" He stood there bobbing his small chin. For a moment I thought he might bark.

"Yes," I repeated. "My father and moth –"

There was a peculiar look about the tiny face, and the bright blue eyes seemed to see me for the first time as he interrupted me.

"Eye-tal-yan?" he repeated softly. "Hmmmm."

With that last observation the shiny, brown lounging slippers were put into slow motion again and the old man shuffled in the direction of a nearby intersection. As he moved away I thought I heard him say it one more time, softly – "Eye-tal-yan" – but I couldn't be sure.

I watched him until he reached the other side of the intersection, then I turned in the direction from which he'd come. The sidewalk was empty, silent.

Maybe tomorrow, I thought, the show will go on.

If it doesn't rain.

# DOVIE

Petite, white-haired, blue-eyed, and fragile with age during my visit with her, she was but a child of five when her parents picked up stakes and moved from rural Doolittle Mills in Perry County to French Lick. When later her father took over the operation of the French Lick Springs Hotel dairy farm, the move became for the little country girl a fantasy come true.

It began with a friendship of mutual fondness and respect with the legendary entrepreneur and hotel owner Tom Taggart Sr. It ended after she spent fifteen unforgettable years as a telephone operator at the hotel's switchboard. Between the two she was showered with wonders of which most girls of her time could only dream, and when she left there she took with her a pocketful of lasting memories.

Her name was Dovie, and as she remembered them, her years at the once popular hotel were radiant with early 20th Century faces of the rich and famous from around the nation and the world. One was Al Smith, who in the late 1920's unsuccessfully challenged Herbert Hoover for the presidency of the United States. As late as my visit with her so many years later she was still convinced he would have made a great president.

She had added, "He was a fine fellow and I voted for

him." There was a cowboy movie star, too, named Tom Mix, who was a frequent hotel visitor. "He wore a business suit, high boots and a ten gallon hat," she said of him. And there were former Indiana Governor Paul V. McNutt, Franklin D. Roosevelt (long before he became president), Thomas Meehan and Irene Castle.

"I saw Miss Castle dance in the lobby with her husband, and she wore such a beautiful gown," she cooed.

"I can't begin to tell you all the famous people I saw there," Dovie shook her head. "On Kentucky Derby weekends they'd come by the hundreds in railroad sleeper cars, and they'd stay at the hotel and go from there to Churchill Downs the next day. My biggest thrill was when I placed a call from the hotel for my movie idol, Douglas Fairbanks, to Mary Pickford, in Hollywood. That was the greatest thrill of my life."

Dovie remembered a thirty-five dollar tip given her by a Capone mobster who honeymooned at the hotel and whose bride wore a pair of $2,200 slippers with golden heels. "A few months later I read where he was shot to death in Chicago," she said.

"You know," she confided proudly, "I placed the first telephone call ever that went from the hotel to Cuba. Oh, it was such a wonderful, exciting place to work. You'd go to work broke and come home with twenty or thirty dollars in tips. Only those people with money went there."

There were several hotels in French Lick at the time. One, Dovie said, in which many gamblers convened, was the Brown Hotel, and five other lesser hotels, and the largest, where she worked, which had more than seven hundred rooms.

"Mr. Taggart was one of the finest men I ever knew," she continued. "If he met you one time he never forgot your name; year after year he'd remember. He used to put five dollar bills in the leaves on the hotel grounds so that the caretakers could find them."

She recalled the times Taggart had related to her and other hotel employees how when he was first married he earned only seven dollars a week.

"He liked to tell that story, and he told it many times," she said.

She remembered, too, that the paternal hotel owner addressed the girls who worked for him as his girlfriends. Once, when Dovie scolded him, "a married man" with so many girlfriends, he laughingly replied, "It's all right, Dovie. Mrs. Taggart doesn't mind if I have lots of girlfriends. But when I have just one, then, Mrs. Taggart says, I'll be in trouble."

Switchboard operators alternated schedules Dovie described as "long and short weeks." They were paid thirteen dollars and fifty cents for a long week, and eleven dollars and seventy-five cents for a short one. "It was a good job, and that was good money for then," Dovie observed. "Then we had our tips. And we had two weeks for vacation."

It was at the hotel that Dovie was smitten by a doorman named Rolla Dillard, and one January day they exchanged marriage vows. Though they were to have no children they did have one of those "I wouldn't change a thing" kind of marriages, Dovie said. In the late years of their long marriage, Rolla had a stroke and required more care than Dovie could physically provide.

Forced to give up their home, they moved into the Paoli Convalescent Center. Dovie was approaching ninety-two at this time and Rolla would catch up twelve days later. My last visit with them had come just a few days short of their seventieth wedding anniversary.

A man told me one time that the lonesomest thing in the whole world is someone who has grown old enough to have outlived family and friends. There is no one left to love, he said, no one to visit, talk with, get letters from or write to.

He knew whereof he spoke for he was old and had outlived his family and friends. That, despite the wonderful long life they had together, is how it was for Dovie and Rolla. But she loved him more than she ever did. Ditto for him too, except that the stroke had left him speechless and he was unable to say so. He made unintelligible sounds which she seemed to understand. But he was recovering, or so it was believed. With the aid of a walker he was able to walk a little, at least enough to use the bathroom.

They had a large bright room at the center, twin beds and some furniture from the home that they sold. They had a single relative, Dovie's niece. Sometimes she or a friend took them by automobile to a store. Some young men from their church picked them up when they were able to go to Sunday service. Dovie's hair dresser would drive down from Orleans and take her back to her shop to fix Dovie's hair. Then she'd bring her back to the convalescent home.

After I had written a column about Dovie and Rolla some long lost friends visited them. The following Christmas some people who must have noted their calendars sent thirty-seven greeting cards. "Thirty-seven," Dovie drew out the number in long accents as though that had been the most magnificent happening of their long life.

Maybe it was. When you're almost ninety-two and have outlived family and friends, who knows? Because of poor eyesight she was unable to read them (at this time she couldn't see well enough to enjoy television) and someone at the center had to read them to her. They were nice people, those employees at the convalescent center, but you'll hear more about them shortly.

Although this particular visit had also resulted in a newspaper column, it was not intended. I decided to write it after Dovie had divulged an unusual encounter to me, and I wanted to share it with my readers. Now I'd like to share it with you. It occurred one night after her heart began beating out of sync.

"It pounded so hard it shook the bed," she spoke in little gasps as the memory came back to her. "Then it began skipping beats, and then it would stop, then start up again. I was sure I was going to die."

She was so sure of her own impending death, she said, "That I spoke to the Lord. I told Him, 'Lord, I've been waiting a long time for this. I want to tell You how much I love You, and how much I appreciate what You've done for Rollie and me down through the years since You saved us.'"

For the record she interrupted her prayer to remind her Lord of a couple of dates. "'You saved me in 1930, when I was twenty-nine years old, and You saved Rollie Sept. 6, 1937. I was so happy,'" she remembered saying.

"I'd have gone to hell if I had died before then," she told me. "I had a very bad temper. I hated, too. I once told a man to drop dead. And when one of our neighbors shot his wife I told my mother, 'It's a shame he didn't kill her,' I was so mean. After I got saved I went to her and apologized and asked her to forgive me. She did and we became the best of friends. I'll tell you, when the Lord fixes you He fixes you up right."

Dovie said she had tried to be saved a number of times before then, but it just hadn't taken.

"Several times I got in touch with the Lord," she said. "Trouble was I wasn't putting Him first. They say salvation is cheap. It is not. It costs you everything you have. You've got to give your all. Jesus lives in my heart because I let Him."

Dovie was prepared to depart this world the night her heart went on a tear. But in the face of the ecstacy she believed awaited her she became selfish, she said.

"And I told the Lord I was, too, and that I was disappointed in myself for being that way. I told Him, 'I want to live long enough to see that Rollie is taken care of.' I said, 'They'll do everything for him here at this convalescent center, I know. They're so wonderful. Everybody hugs and kisses you and loves you, and they take such good care of you, and the food is good. I've never seen anything like it in all of my life. But I want to take care of Rollie myself, like I've always done, until You take him. Then I'll come along.'"

A lady with a sensible request can be awfully hard to turn down. Or maybe it was the intervention of the nice people at the center. In either case, Dovie's Lord did not take her away that night. Neither did she get her wish. Her Lord had other plans and rather unexpectedly He stopped at the convalescent center for a second or two one day and they left there together.

Rolla was without her for the first time in more than seventy years. But not for long, for he soon followed his dear wife. However, during the remainder of his life the employees at the center, as Dovie had suspected, lovingly cared for him.

# LOST CEMETERY

What is it that people never stop to think about when they're enjoying summer fun on Lake Monroe, or, for that matter, when they are gulping a refreshing glass of water from that reservoir?

Answer?

The peaceful rest of hundreds of dead in seven burial grounds was disturbed to make it all possible.

There were eight burial grounds in the way of development and slated for removal when it was decided to build the lake.

But even with the aid of next of kin, the U. S. Army Corps of Engineers, after exhausting investigation, could find only seven.

Is it possible that a cemetery can be lost?

"It's possible," said Heltonville mortician Dwight Jones. "There's no way of knowing how many burial grounds have been lost.

"You're probably not aware of it," he offered, "but there was a time when people didn't travel very far to bury their dead. And over the years graves get grown over from lack of care, and in time they are lost."

Yeah, but these are modern times, and there'd be gravestones. They'd be around.

"Let me tell you something," Jones removed the cigar he was puffing on from his mouth. "Stones will disappear, get knocked over and buried. Sometimes they're carried away.

"When an old barn was torn down to make way for the lake at Paynetown," he continued, "it was discovered that the cornerstone pillars were old broken tombstones, installed face down so that the inscriptions could not be seen."

Jones and his father, Leston Jones, operated the Jones Funeral Home in Heltonville. The father-son team had a long established reputation for integrity, care and understanding. And in that part of rural Indiana where the sparsely settled corners of Monroe, Lawrence and Jackson counties are joined, the Jones mortuary firm, founded in 1928 by Leston, had long been accepted as family.

When cemeteries were removed from the lake construction area in the early 1960's, the daily attendance of a mortician as an observer was required. When he was approached by the Corps of Engineers to act in that capacity, Jones said to himself, "Why not? It might be the chance of a lifetime."

The experience may not have been that rewarding, but it was an interesting one, and for no more than "just observing," the job paid thirty dollars a day.

"Contrary to all that's been said about how deep they used to bury the dead, the remains in those cemeteries were buried no deeper than five feet," Jones revealed one lesson the experience taught him. "I know, because I measured. There were none at six feet."

It was also interesting to note that none of the seven cemeteries was removed by excavating machinery or machinery of any kind.

"It was all done by hand by a civil contractor and his

crew with picks and shovels," Jones said of the manner in which the task was completed. "And the remains from each grave were put into a wooden box three feet long, eighteen inches wide and a foot high."

It was in this manner that the total of three hundred forty-one disinterments were made from the seven cemeteries. Those burial grounds included the Daniel Fox Cemetery, Russell Mitchell Cemetery, Blackwell Cemetery, Hughes Cemetery, Macy W. Malott Cemetery, Goodman Cemetery and Shields Cemetery.

The cemetery that couldn't be found was the Cutright Cemetery. The Corps of Engineers made a thorough search, next of kin were called in, but all efforts to locate the old burial ground were in vain.

"Some of those cemeteries that were relocated would never have been reached by lake water, but it was cheaper for the government to move them than it was to build a road into them," Jones said. "But no one knows where the lost one is."

Of the total disinterments, only two bodies, buried some four decades earlier, were found in sealed vaults. These were removed and reinterred intact with the aid of a crane. That same method unfortunately crushed some concrete vaults, until Jones devised a way to lift them from their resting places with the aid of timbers.

Two disinterments were reinterred in Clear Creek Cemetery at Harrodsburg at the request of next of kin. The remaining three hundred thirty-nine were transported to Allens Creek and reinterred in a site that was purchased specifically for relocating the cemeteries.

According to the Corps of Engineers, the project was begun on October 6, 1964, and was completed May 1, 1965. Before removals were made, next of kin were advised and invited to attend both the disinterment and reinterment.

At the conclusion of the project, the new burial site at Allens Creek, situated on a hillside that rises from the gravel road that leads to the Allens Creek Launch Ramp, was deeded to the Polk Township Trustee.

"A disinterment and reinterment had to be made in one day," the mortician recalled a stipulation of the removal process. "Remains were uncovered, boxed and buried all the same day. No remains were allowed to be left out of the ground overnight."

The civil contractor employed eight or more men for the project. Jones remembered that they worked slowly and carefully at the task.

"I know that when they found remains they removed them all, and, if it was there, they even put the stone marker in the box," he said.

"But as far as the lost cemetery is concerned," Jones shook his head, "they couldn't find it. It's still there someplace."

# THE CAMP

Homer looked at the big watch on the end of a long chain he had fished out from the bib-pocket of his overalls and said it was time for lunch. He straightened up from where we were sitting on the old bench and pushed open a rusty corrugated metal door. Almost blinded by the burst of tawny sunshine that greeted us we stepped out of the tiny cabin into the quiet hollow and a raw March noontime.

Mutt ran playfully down from a hillside and dogged his master's heels. They moved slowly over the foot-log that spanned the deep, wide bed of the dry branch. It was almost too quiet. Because of the warming sunshine, the maple sap, frozen in the jutting spires earlier that morning, now dripped freely into large five-gallon cans hanging on the trees under them. Homer stopped and turned to me.

"The season has got to be right for making syrup," he said. "You gotta have freezin' and thawin' and then the water (sap) runs good. You can figure about the first of February to start. I have started as much as a week or two 'fore that. But it's usually about the first of February."

The morning trek to the log cabin, "The Camp," as

Homer called it, followed the dry wash. Now, for the quarter-mile walk back to the house, we glided through a field of burnished grass made golden by the sunshine. As we walked I began reviewing my morning back there at The Camp. The first thing that had caught my eye was an old coffee pot sitting on the furnace.

"Hot drink?" I had asked hopefully.

Homer laughed at my question and said, "Nope. Just keep it there for the homey feeling. It's full of nails."

Three sides of the silver poplar and oak log cabin I noticed were chinked. The insides of the walls were lined with the flattened-out jackets of discarded water heaters. There was no chinking, and nothing lined the inside of the wall built around and over the flue-end of the furnace. Steam from three large old-fashioned round black kettles and a smaller oblong kettle built into the top of the furnace billowed up and through the openings between the logs. The vats were filled with boiling sap.

"This is the third cabin I've built on this spot," Homer Spriggs was saying as he pushed a long log into the fire. "This here furnace is about ten feet or more from this fire door to the flue out there. Built right on mother earth."

Field stones, and mud, dried hard from many fires, were the only components of the furnace, and a scrap of sheet metal served as its door.

"The gables are logged, take a look. See?" Homer continued, "and those are rib-poles up there," with a gesture he had directed my attention upward, "with the metal roof spread over them."

The heat from the furnace was comforting, but the wall which served as a back-rest to the bench on which we sat was cold. The earth under our feet was cold too, and I was cold, and if the water was not running very fast from the sugar maples on the wintry hillsides it at least was running freely from my nose.

"Who d'yuh think built it?" Homer was saying. "I built every speck of it. I built the first one more'n fifty years ago. Been making syrup here since. But, my daddy boiled water here long, long before I was born in 1886. He boiled it down near the house. He didn't make syrup though. They'd let it go to sugar. That's how they got their sugar back then."

He'd said he was eighty-one. It was hard to believe. Under the bib-overalls, overalls jacket, sweater, plaid shirt, ankle-high shoes covered with two-buckle rubber boots, there certainly could not have been an old man. He was a man who'd not only gotten up before five o'clock that morning, but a man who also had cooked his own breakfast, and that of Icis, his wife, did his chores and then trudged an icy quarter-mile up the branch to The Camp.

White hair stuck out from below his red and black cap. The inside ear-tip band was pulled down for warmth but the hound dog flaps remained tied up, with a black bow on the top. From behind a pair of smudged spectacles shone unusually bright smiling blue eyes which must have been connected to his vocal chords for every word he uttered was riddled with smiles. Big, wrinkled, almost gnarled hands appeared as though they had been made especially for many of the words he spoke.

He talked of friends from "those good old days," many of whom he said were gone. They were the children and grandchildren of the original settlers of the Benton Township area situated off Brummetts Creek Road less than a mile from the Brown County line.

"I've set here many an hour," he spat into the dirt

floor and paused to run the back of his hand across his mouth. "I think about the neighbors. And I think about the good old days. We had a lot of fun then."

He talked about his past, and his family, and in the stillness of the surrounding hollow outside, interrupted only by the distant sound of an airplane motor high in the air, echoes of Noble and Mable, his children filled the tiny woodland cabin.

"They used to help me a lot in here when they was young," he said almost sadly.

Homer moved to the storage tank and began dipping fresh sap from it through a large cloth strainer into a big container. When it was filled he moved to the long furnace with it in his hands.

"Now you see, you can't put this cold water in the boiling kettles," he cautioned me as though I might have done it. "It'll cool them off too much. You have to heat it first. So you put it right here in the heater."

He poured the contents of the can into the oblong vessel built into the front top of the furnace. Then he was reaching for an old-fashioned drinking dipper fastened to a long shiny black-oak stick.

"My daddy made this, and he's been dead thirty-five years," he informed me. "See how slick and shiny this handle is. That's from use. When the water gets to boiling too much you cool it with this dipper, see?"

He dipped up some of the boiling sap and then poured it back into the kettle from a great height. He repeated this several times and the foamy turbulence in the kettle abated.

"See this bench you're settin' on?" he asked. "That's one board. White oak. I cut that myself. Now just look at that. How much planing do you think it would take to make that smooth? Isn't that a piece of sawing?"

Although he had a chew of tobacco in his mouth he

reached to a corner of the bench and held up a large capped jar.

"I smoke a pipe and I keep an extra one right in here along with my tobacco and chewing, see?" he said. "Got it right here when I want it."

Comfortable on the bench Homer wanted to talk. He told me a story. The previous summer while he was pruning a tree in his front yard a cut branch fell to the ground and landed near a rattlesnake a few feet from him.

Homer called his wife out to the porch so she could see it and he told her, "Boy, I'm going to catch that thing and put it in a barrel, and when people come around I'll really have something to show them."

Well, it didn't take but a couple seconds and Homer learned who was boss of the rattlesnakes in his part of the county.

"You put that thing in a barrel and I'll take off down that lane and never come back," his wife threatened.

That did it. Homer shot the head off the snake and put the long carcass in a pasteboard box along with one fang he recovered from the shooting scene. He put the whole business in a shed.

Despite my objections, Homer insisted on being a good host and showed me the snake. Good grief! That thing was as big around as my trembling wrist and had eighteen rattles on it. Still spookier was that Homer had shaped a viper head from a piece of wood, drew two eyes and a mouth on it with crayon, then fastened his work of art to the dead carcass.

Dead as it was, all coiled up in that pasteboard box with that vicious looking head on it, and the single fang resting on top the head, at the sight of it I very nearly jumped out of my skin. I couldn't begin to describe the sensation that went all up and down my back but oh, how I could feel it. That snake couldn't have been more alive as far as I was concerned and it was a relief when Homer put it back in the shed. When he locked the door I was especially relieved, knowing that dead snake wasn't going to somehow be resurrected and come crawling out of there.

The kettles had begun roiling up again and Homer reached for a homemade fan, a large piece of stiff cardboard fastened to a long stick. He waved it at the kettles from where he sat on the bench. Again the churning sap subsided into a hot bubbling. He said there were thirty-eight gallons of tree water in the kettles and in the heater. And he made the surprising announcement that fifty gallons of the water were needed to obtain one gallon of maple syrup.

The many hours he worked in the tiny cabin were spent there more for pleasure than profit. His tireless efforts were rewarded with a few pint jars of maple syrup each week which he sold to the half-dozen or so customers on his egg route. What was left over usually was sold to friends.

"Yep. Made this all myself," he repeated. And he added, "That furnace wasn't built in any new-fangled way. Just put stones right on top of the ground and chinked them with clay. I was here about nine o'clock last night to put a night-stick in there."

He went outside and returned with a long pole-like log. He rested one end on the dirt floor and drew back the sheet metal furnace door. Then he fed the long stick into the blaze under the boiling kettles. Turning his attention elsewhere he began dipping water from the heater into the kettles. He followed this by straining fresh sap from the tank and refilling the heater.

"I had five brothers and a sister," he volunteered.

"They're all dead now except my sister, Ella. Ella Carpenter. She's about ninety-four, now, and living in Tucson.

"My brother George lived right square north of here on that point," he continued, extending a finger toward the wooden door at the opposite end of the small cabin. "He was a musician. I don't guess I was over sixteen and I got him to send for me a guitar. His wife gave me lessons on it. Many's the time me and a neighbor boy would entertain the folks around here with guitar and banjo music from eight o'clock 'way into the night."

Homer lapsed into a solemn mood.

"I'd like to see Ella again," he mused. "Yep. I'd like to see her mighty well. Sometimes I have the notion just to pull out and go see her."

Most of the quarter-mile walk from The Camp was behind us. Mutt was running well ahead. We'd passed an old, unused fallen-down saw mill. Inside was a rusted 1926 model 10&20 McCormick Deering tractor. Then we passed an old blacksmith shop, its forge lifeless and cold. Mutt, the handsome golden-brown mongrel, had tagged along, rubbing against our legs wanting to play. Giving up he ran well ahead, nosing first into one place then another making as much noise as a herd of cattle as he bounded among the crisp leaves. Homer checked some buckets and showed me how to make spires, the spigot-like tubes hammered into trees that dripped sap into the buckets.

We'd crossed the second foot-log over the wash and Homer recalled how he'd cut the tree, stripped and hewed the log and placed it where it was. In front of the house with its "up-and-down twelve-inch sealed poplar siding" and black roll-paper roof, Homer stopped.

"This house was built eighty-two years ago," he said. "I was born in this house."

He sounded as though his voice was bent under a weight of memories, like the old unpainted picket fence around the house was bent.

Driving away from there, along the lane flanked by trees whose branches interlocked overhead, I remembered what Icis had said earlier about that very spot.

"It is beautiful in the summer, when the leaves are green. It's like a beautiful canopy." She smiled wanly and added, "I used to call it lover's lane, until I got too old."

As I continued driving I thought about the little cabin in the sun-filled hollow. When I looked back steam from the kettles escaping from every opening almost covered it until it seemed to be disappearing in the mists of another time.

# THE DREAM

It was believed, at least by them, that if minus twenty degree temperatures and swirling flood waters couldn't dislodge Raymond and Sarah Ashby from their snug retreat on the east bank of White River, near Worthington, nothing could, and Sarah underscored that belief with straightforward candor.

"You couldn't pull me away," she said.

And with reference to the Ashby's former home, she added, "You couldn't pull me back to Indianapolis either. When I have to go there I find so much more traffic, so much confusion, so many people, and so many cars in the parking lots."

The Ashbys had left the capital city ten years earlier, after Raymond retired at sixty from a die-setting job at General Motors, and after Sarah drew the curtain on a procession of work years that included stints with RCA, Stuart Warner and Indiana Bell Telephone Company.

"We had fished here for about eight years before that," Raymond recalled their decision to make their new home on the river. "We both enjoyed fishing, and fish, and this is the place we wanted to do it."

Their home was a two-bedroom, completely modern, small but cozy frame. Immediately upon entering I was envious of them and found myself wishing the place were mine.

"It's big enough for us, but when all the kids are here," she broke into a laugh and shook her head from side to side, "we have a lot of company. Then," she sighed pleasantly, "it's pretty small."

The Ashbys had three sons and a daughter – and fifteen grandchildren and five great grandchildren who loved to visit Grandfather and Grandmother at their river home. To accommodate the swell of numbers, the Ashbys had attached a 20 X 10 foot patio to the back side of the house, overlooking the river.

"They enjoy that thing," Raymond smiled. As an afterthought he added, "We all do, as a matter of fact."

After settling themselves on the river bank a decade earlier, the Ashbys turned their major physical efforts toward the river – fishing.

"A feller," Raymond explained with a wink, "has got to have something to do in his spare time."

Fishing was more than that to the couple. Early on it became a means of supplementing shrinking retirement income. Catches were frozen and offered for sale. White perch, catfish, buffalo, sturgeon, and quillback. The couple's popularity began to increase. Their daughter decided they should call their snug aerie "The Whale House" and post a sign to identify it as such. That is how I was able to find the place.

Thus a fish business, on a small scale, was launched. Raymond and Sarah used D-nets aided by a few trotlines to catch the quantities of fish that were in demand. Fishing took them two miles up-river and two miles down-river, and they enjoyed every minute of it. Fish business? It was one of those millions of American dreams you hear about. With a little daring it had come true.

Dreams are woven from microscopic strands of angel hair and the delicate glistenings of early morning dew, and as such are vulnerable to disaster. Raymond's and Sarah's was not to be an exception. The end came about in this way:

"People began coming from all over the state," Raymond recounted the growing demand for river fish. "Weekdays, Saturdays, Sundays. They really like those fish," he said.

The Ashby's sold as much as four hundred pounds to one caller. Another three hundred pounds were sold to one family for canning. "They got ninety-four quarts out of that mess," Raymond said.

Usually the amounts per sale were smaller. In ten years, however, the total amount of fish sold from The Whale House was startling.

"We used to love to eat fish," Sarah began revealing the first half of the Ashby dream that had disintegrated. "It was just so good to sit down to a mess. But," she scrunched up her face, "not anymore.

"We have cleaned and filleted so many fish that we have lost our taste for them. And," she raised her voice slightly in warning, "if you ever clean as many fish as we have cleaned you won't eat them anymore either."

Raymond agreed.

"I have to blame the cleaning of them for my loss of taste for fish," he said. "I used to just simply love them."

Except for that tragedy, the remainder of the Ashby dream remained intact – for a while.

"We have no regrets," Raymond said, "We have more fun here than you can shake a stick at."

Sarah hurried to agree.

Their fun times on the river included the unusually

cold, blowy, snowy winter of 1977-78, and the flooding that followed.

"I have a photograph of the thermometer out there on that tree," Sarah said with a gesture, "while it registered twenty-degrees below zero."

She forthwith produced it, along with several other color shots of a frozen river, acres of white, white snow, and a sea that had escaped the river's banks and surrounded the Ashby home and the homes of their neighbors who shared the river bank with them. The deep freeze had turned the river into a solid mass. Snow was everywhere, deep, crippling.

"We couldn't get out for a few days," Raymond said. "But we were all right."

When the ice and snow melted, the river rose higher than the high bank on which the couple's house was built. It surrounded the house. It rushed to cover all the farmland in sight, and nearby State Road 157, isolating the old iron bridge across the river there. One of the photographs that Sarah proffered showed a neighbor and his wife on their way across what had to be a field, on their way to their own house, in a boat powered by an outboard.

"Didn't scare us out," Sarah said defiantly.

When they weren't fishing, the Ashbys traveled to several states, including Hawaii by plane, and to Florida by car. After some health problems – not serious – Sarah stopped fishing altogether and began working with ceramics. She was able to build up a sizeable following which had increased steadily through word of mouth recommendations.

Good thing. For a few months preceding my visit the fish hadn't been biting, and the Ashbys – The Whale House, as Raymond put it – were "bought out of fish." But if that constituted another disaster the Ashbys must have been keeping it a secret.

"We're still having fun," Raymond said.

"Yes," nodded Sarah. "And you couldn't pull me out of here."

Perhaps not. But there came a day when the river bank where the Whale House once stood was bare. The abodes of neighboring river dwellers were gone. Giant earth-moving machines charged to and fro, the boom of a tall crane sliced through the morning sunlight, men in hard hats moved about. The entire river bank had become part of a flood control project that included replacement of the old iron bridge on State Road 157. The place was unrecognizable.

The disaster was complete.

The dream ended.

# THE LETTER

There was no music, no confetti, no glamour. Just a simple reading of the vows of matrimony: The promises – until death. Death. The very sound of the word rang bitterly of irony, for it was death that had landed him in jail. It was death that was now sending him far away from his tearful new bride, far away for two to twenty-one years.

A sheriff's deputy was preparing him for the transfer from the county jail to the state prison. He stood there squinting his eyes as though each question brought new pain. His answers came slowly, thoughtfully, with a minimum of words and less clarity. He appeared to have difficulty remembering.

"I don't know if I'm guilty. I don't guess I'll never know," he told me, squinting his eyes repeatedly.

The strange reflex caused his nose and upper cheeks to quiver. In his shirt pocket he carried a letter from the woman he'd married. The ceremony had taken place only steps away from where he now stood. A justice of the peace had tied the knot. Witnesses were relatives and friends of the bride.

He touched the letter with a hand. Maybe it was a caress; a tender press with the flat of his hand. He did not read it. He couldn't. He had never learned to read. He could not write.

"I never went to school," he confided half apologetical-ly, half matter of factly. "I don't know why. I think I had pneumonia or something like that when I was a kid. And I couldn't go."

He earlier had asked me to read it to him. It was a farewell note from his new wife.

"I know what a good husband you're going to be when you come home," she had written. "The kids are sure excited about going to be with you. Try to think of what's ahead of you. Just think of all the good times we have had, and will again when you get back. And pray a lot for guidance and protection from all evil things around you."

He had pleaded guilty to involuntary manslaughter in the death of his friend.

"My lawyer told me I'd get life if I went to trial. He said if I didn't plead guilty I was sure to get a life sentence." His eyes squinted, and his nose and upper cheeks twitched in time to the words as they left his lips.

"It was a drunken fight," he continued. "We were friends. We always drank together. Like I told them in court, I don't know that I even hit him."

He admitted having been arrested and jailed a number of times for fighting before that. One time for theft.

His left hand reached to the breast pocket of his shirt again – the letter. His thumb hooked over the edge of the pocket as a finger moved gently over the paper on which his new bride had inked her affections.

"My darling sweetheart," she had written. "I'm going to save some money for us to spend when you get home. Honey, there is no way our marriage will ever be undone, because I'm going to be the kind of wife I should."

Time was growing short. The deputy was prepared to begin the long automobile journey to the state prison.

"Me and him always drank together," the prisoner felt compelled to resume his account of his unclear memoir.

"But we never fought. I didn't know we had a fight until I woke up. I don't know that I even hit him. I was drunk. I didn't know he was dead until I woke up. It was me that called the law. I probably hit him, but I don't remember. I don't know if I'm guilty."

He stood quietly for a few moments. His eyes closed and opened at a furious rate. He needed to speak.

"My lawyer first wanted me to take fifteen to twenty-five years in prison," he remembered. "I told him I couldn't do that. I suppose I ought to serve two or three years. I told him this was an accident. I'm willing to do two or three years. Sometimes I thought the lawyer was trying to help me, and other times I thought he wasn't. The court gave him to me. I couldn't hire a lawyer. My boss said my lawyer was not trying to help me. A deputy here at the jail told me the same thing."

He raised his left hand to his shirt pocket. The letter. Pressing his palm to it he seemed to take courage from it.

"Just by marrying me," the words of his wife in the letter under his hand continued, "you have made me happier than I have ever been . . ."

He gave his age as thirty-eight. The man he was alleged to have killed in a drunken fight – his friend –was fifty-seven.

"No," he said, "I don't remember. He was dead, and they said I did it. Maybe I did. But I don't remember. I guess I'll never know."

In quiet tones the deputy notified him that it was time to leave.

"All right," the prisoner replied, blinking his eyes at that same rapid pace. "All right, I'm ready."

He looked at his new wife, at the gathering. He raised his cuffed hands and placed one over the pocket of his shirt – the letter.

"Good-bye," he said.

# OLD JOSH

Physically challenged since birth, old Josh was unable to stand erect. He could see forward only if he forced his eyebrows upward. And then his brow was creased by deep furrows, giving it the appearance of a washboard. When he walked his right shoe dragged with a scraping sound.

Josh was the swamper in a tavern owned by Biddy's father. It was his primary mission to keep the place clean. Armed with broom, mop and bucket, he would suddenly appear at closing time. When he at last retired for the night the barroom was left groomed and orderly.

Early mornings found him behind the bar tacitly serving haggard and trembling addicts who took their needed shots from the wizened swamper in shaking hands. Because he rarely encouraged conversation, few of them ever spoke to Josh. He worked silently until up in the morning when Biddy's father came down from the apartment over the tavern to relieve him. Usually just before lunch.

Biddy's father had arranged a corner of a storeroom at the rear of the tavern to serve as Josh's home. It wasn't much, as abodes go, but it was the only home the old man had. And it was in that corner that Josh spent almost all of his free time.

Biddy, who was without siblings, was also handicapped since birth. After seeing his daughter as helpless as a newly hatched nestling, Biddy's father swore that there would never be another child born to him and his wife. He blamed God for Biddy's condition, and his unceasing anger and heartache left him drawn and morose. He loved the child very much and he often secretly wept at her plight. Frail and deformed, she fortunately could see, but she could not speak. She made gurgling sounds that came always from a gaping, drooling mouth in a constantly distorted face. And she could not hear.

It was like a hot dagger in Biddy's father's heart when people shrank from the sight of the child. As a consequence of that he kept Biddy hidden from view, taking an oath to himself that no one should ever again look inhumanely upon his helpless daughter.

When the weather was warm Biddy's father would take his tiny daughter in his arms and carry her down to the small yard behind the barroom. To assure privacy he had it enclosed with a high board fence. Lying on a cot, protected from curious eyes by this screen, Biddy, usually with her mother seated lovingly beside her, would spend long hours there.

At those times Biddy also had a visitor. Old Josh would sit at her side and speak soft, simple, affectionate words to her. With a long bony finger coarsened by time and labor, he would playfully chuck her under the chin or push back a wisp of hair from her forehead. When they were in bloom in beds around the perimeter of the yard, he would bring her flowers.

One day as the child seemed to be watching and listening intently, Josh spent long, long minutes explaining in detail to Biddy the two halves of a robin's blue egg he held gently cupped in a gnarled hand. Softly he explained from whence they had come, that a life had been created inside them, and how that life had eventually come into the world to make it a brighter, happier and euphonious place.

In response to his attentions Biddy made meaningless sounds and twisted her face into a grotesque smile. Although she could not hear she seemed to understand his every word. Josh would chuckle warmly within himself and though no one could see them, his eyes would brighten.

Before leaving her he would kneel by Biddy's cot and, with ancient, loving lips buss the child on the cheek, or the forehead, or even on her gaping, drooling mouth. He would then laugh in his chuckling way and wave goodbye as he walked away in that bent and awkward gait of his.

One morning at breakfast Biddy's mother told her husband that she believed Biddy understood everything old Josh ever said to the child. "I just know she does," she said to Biddy's father. "Don't ask me how I know. I just know."

It was mid-June, a few months after her seventh birthday, when Biddy died. No one knew how Josh got to the cemetery on the day of her funeral. Biddy's father and mother felt a crush of remorse when they saw him, for in their bereavement and grief they had forgotten the old swamper.

Josh stood there silently but conspicuous in an old wrinkled blue suit, un-ironed white shirt buttoned at the collar and no tie. He listened passively as a priest intoned some prayers and gave the final blessing.

Then, dragging the toe of his right foot, Josh moved

toward the grave. He limped slowly, head down, eyes straining upward to better see the small white coffin that held the body of the little girl. He stood there looking at it for long moments. He might have wept, but he had used up all his tears when as a boy, because of his own physical condition, his eyes had secretly bled them nightly into his pillow. As Biddy's father and mother, and other mourners, watched, Josh extended a hoary fist and placed something on the coffin lid.

The gathered mourners watched as Josh made an about face and without a word limped away, dragging that foot as always. When they returned their attention to Biddy's casket they saw what the old man had placed on it. There on the polished white surface next to a spray of red roses bearing a wide ribbon on which gold letters spelled out "Father & Mother," Josh had placed two halves of a robin's blue egg.

That was many years ago and Biddy's father and mother, their aching hearts stilled, are now at rest near Biddy. Her mother lived only months after her daughter's passing. But for years until his death Biddy's white-haired father would find himself wondering what happened to old Josh after he left the cemetery the day of Biddy's funeral.

# SAVORY INDIANA

When the first October sun turns the morning dew into diamond brilliancy and the wind is brisk as menthol aftershave on your cheeks, you can pick any one of numerous rural south central Indiana roads that rise easily and fall lazily around winding curves, and find the comfort of a dream, and real people to fill it. That's how I got to Elwren one morning long ago and found Earl and Irene Whaley and Allie and Ethel Sparks.

There really wasn't an Elwren anymore. There were about as many homes in the area as there ever were, maybe more, but the Elwren of a half century earlier had disappeared into the past. Standing with one foot on a rick of wood and the other on the flat bed of a truck I listened to the Whaleys and the Sparkses speak of that Elwren of another time. I heard them tell of how the one-room Blair School building, which was erected in Blair Hollow about a mile northeast of where we stood, was moved by pulling it with a team of horses to the intersection of Elwren Road and the road that leads down into Stanford.

Allie flagged Illinois Central trains that day as the building, on long planks and rollers, was moved across the three rail lines that used to parallel Elwren Road. Two of those lines were gone when I visited there, and so was the Elwren School. That was the name they gave it after relocating the one-room structure.

Lucy Rowe and Charlie Hudson were two of the teachers who came to memory as having taught in the old school. They used polk-berry ink in school in those days. John Ellen was the owner of Blair Hollow. the first site of the school. Those were the days, too, when only a few people had Delco plants for generating electricity in their homes. Most of them used coal oil (kerosene) lamps and lanterns for light, and Allie Sparks worked as a section hand on the IC for a dollar and fifty cents a day.

There were unhappy times in Elwren, too, such as the time Tanny Walker was killed while loading logs on an IC flatcar, and Andy Walker was killed by an IC train at the grade crossing nearby, and when a young man shot to death his step-father.

There was a happy day of note.

"That was about 1922," recalled Earl Whaley, "when they piked this road. Before that it was just a muddy mess, and in the winter time we couldn't get out of here."

Three years later Earl Whaley drove the first Elwren school bus, a Model-T Ford, carrying Elwren youngsters to Bloomington High School. He was to drive a school bus twenty-one years before he quit. At the time of my visit two school buses plied the roadway carrying children to and from Grandview School and the junior and senior high schools in Bloomington.

The IC Railroad at one time maintained a depot in Elwren. It was the nearest rail freight pickup station to Hendricksville, and each day a wagon loaded with merchandise pulled by a team of horses arrived in Elwren from Hendricksville and was unloaded at the general store. People poured out of the hills and hollows of the countryside to board one or the other of the east-west passenger trains that clackety-clacked over the main lines twice each day. At evening time they would return to disembark from the trains and disappear into the anonymity of the life from whence they had come.

As a guest in the Sparks home later that day I was aware of low ceilings, ancient kitchen chairs, trunks, bureaus and metal beds. The heat from a black and nickel plate Florence coal stove made its four rooms lazy and sleepy, its rocking chairs narcotic.

"It's a kind of a poor do with us," said Ethel Sparks from under her colorful dust cap. "But as long as we do for ourselves and not be a bother to anybody else it's better than living someplace else."

At eighty-one she was the oldest woman in attendance at a Sparks family reunion the Sunday before. Allie Sparks, who was the same age, was the oldest man in Elwren.

"We've lived here all our lives," he said of the couple's fifty-nine years of marriage. "And we're going to stay as long as we're able to do for ourselves."

Ethel Sparks spent every spare minute of her time quilting.

"I cook two times a day, and we eat lunch leftovers for supper," she said. "Land, I can't count the number of quilts I've made. Hundreds of them, I guess. If I can keep my fingers busy maybe my hands and arms won't get like my feet and legs are."

One of the more notable people to come out of Elwren was Blutcher Poole, one-time technical secretary of the Indiana State Board of Health. Some notable people stayed on there. Two of them were Earl and Irene Whaley.

"Just before last Mothers Day," Ethel Sparks began recalling one of numerous steps Irene had taken to notability, "She come over and papered this room, and when she was finished she said, 'There, Ethel, there's your Mother's Day present.' It's so nice to have good neighbors."

The IC maintained three lines at Elwren; the main line, a siding, and a spur to the loading dock. Only the main line remained, and high weeds along its bed hid it from view until one either walked or drove under a viaduct built in 1917, or walked over an old wooden bridge from where the vista opened downward on the lonely tracks. All else was gone. The depot, the trains, the passengers, the wagon and team from Hendricksville, the section crew that was stationed nearby, in short, the romance that a complete railroad service once brought to a rural community.

As a boy Earl Whaley, who was sixty-six at the time of this visit in 1970, walked the IC railroad to Solsberry High School long before school buses began hauling youngsters out of Elwren to Bloomington High School. Earl, and Irene, who was fifty-eight, were unloading huge lumps of coal by hand into the Sparks' coal shed when I arrived that morning.

I was incredulous, and I asked, "You haul coal?"

"Once a year," Irene answered. "For them."

Meaning Allie and Ethel.

"They're neighbors," she explained. "We still live where people have neighbors and know who they are."

Allie Sparks was standing on the ground looking up at us, Earl and Irene in the truck bed, and I standing spraddle-legged where I was, and he said, "They's the best you ever lived by, too."

Actually the stone-sided Sparks' house was a healthy walk from the Whaley's, and another house

164

sat between them. But out there, then, you apparently had to be separated by much longer distances before you were out of range of neighborliness.

"I've knowed the boy ever since he was a little kid," Ethel Sparks, a tall heavy woman, spoke sweetly and kindly of Earl Whaley. "After him and her got married she's always been a friend to us. She just calls me Ethel, but so many of the people we know call me Mamaw, and my husband, Papaw."

The Whaleys had brought the load of coal from a Greene County mine the day before. As they continued unloading it we talked, and it was from them that I obtained the following account of Elwren.

"Uncle Bob Fowler had a store here years ago," Earl Whaley said. "From the outside it looked like a coal shed, with only one window and a door. He kept a slab of bacon in there, some tobacco, and some canned goods. There were three other stores. John Ballinger had one that wasn't much better than Fowler's. It was on the other side of the railroad tracks. But he was the undertaker, too. I used to drive his horses that pulled the hearse. They were old, and when they gave out we used to take the logging horse to the hearse.

"The big store was on the south side of the tracks," he continued, "and when the post office came it was put there. It was started by McHaley and Isom. Later they sold to Bill Yoho and Orville Barnes, and finally, Edgar Helms, the depot agent for the IC, bought it. The fourth store was a big general store that was owned by Ezra Dyer."

At the time of my visit there were no stores in Elwren, the nearest being at Stanford. In order to shop, the Sparkses depended on their neighbors to give them a lift there and back. Elwren at one time was something of a turkey producing area. The big holiday birds were dry-picked, packed in barrels, and shipped to numerous destinations, including New York City. A portion of Elwren was in Greene County and the remainder in Monroe County. Passenger trains made it easy for those who lived in Monroe county's part of Elwren to ride to Bloomington to pay their taxes, and they made it just as easy for the people in the other part to ride to Bloomfield to pay theirs. There was no church there; Baptists attended services every two weeks at a church in Stanford. On alternate Sundays, services were held in the nearby Greene County Chapel by Elwren's Methodists.

"We younger people used to walk across fields to both," Earl Whaley laughed. "The old folks went to one or the other, but we'd go to both just to have something to do, just to be going someplace. We had a path wore to both of them."

# FLORA KNIGHT MASTERS

The sites were vacant and lonely, and when she traveled over the countryside Flora Masters encountered difficulty in trying to remember where exactly the old schools stood.

There were in her thirty-two years of teaching, her first school at Friendship. And there was Knight School, where she and her four sisters and one brother had attended classes. And Lampkins, Rush, and Phillips, the last of all of them to be razed.

"And all those people who came to those schools, they're all gone now, too, a lot of them," she mused one morning at her home in Bloomington.

The eldest of the children of Andrew Jackson and Amanda Terrell Knight, Flora, early in life, had set her heart on becoming a teacher. And when she completed the necessary grades at Knight School she took herself off to Central Normal College where she earned her teaching certificate.

A younger sister, Florence Chambers, was to follow in her footsteps.

To teach at those early schools took as much stamina as it did dedication.

"I used to have to walk four and five miles and more every morning and night," she recalled. "That was the worst of it – walking in the mud and rain, and wading water in the creek. It's a wonder I survived."

She did more than survive. At this time Flora was in her ninety-fifth year.

But recalling those struggles to reach her classes, she said, "It'd be hard telling how many miles I walked," and in comparison to other teachers, she said with a nod and a smile, "and I'll bet no teacher around had as much wading and water to cross, as I did. It was a great deal harder than teaching."

In her years at Friendship a distant ford on Salt Creek offered a shortcut home. Often when she arrived there it was to learn that rains above and beyond Friendship had swollen the creek from bank to bank and "I'd have to walk all those miles back to school and take the regular way home, just twice as far as I'd have had to go in the first place," she remembered.

A long narrow photograph on one of her living room walls showed her standing amid a group of almost one hundred educators attending a "Teacher's Institute" at Indiana University at Second and Walnut Streets in Bloomington.

Her attire was much the same as that of the other women in the photo – long skirt, almost to the ground, high waist with a sash to emphasize the bosom, and long hair done neatly atop the head.

"You see how much older teachers were back then," she raised her cane and lifted a tiny, thin finger off the grip to point. "See those old faces? You don't see old faces in the schoolrooms now. I think it's better for the children. I've heard children say, 'I don't want to go to school to that teacher. She's old.' When I went to school all teachers were old."

168

There was no objection on her part, however, because, "Going to school was the one thing I wanted to do."

As a girl growing up on a farm, there was more to do than just go to school. "We worked in the fields, and we did all that there was to do on a farm," she said of herself and her sisters and brother.

She left the farm about ten years prior to my visit. "When you leave the farm you leave a lot of work," she said, pleased with her decision to move into the city.

But deeper than that pleasure was the memory of how things were, and how they had changed, and it was at this point that Flora had recalled the vacant, lonely sites of the schools in which she spent more than three decades as a teacher.

"You think back to when you were a child, when you first could remember, and you say to yourself, 'Oh, how things have changed,'" she said.

Church and Sunday School were the week's big events when she was a girl.

"I think it's great that young people can get out now and be with each other," she compared her youth to the current time. "They're so lucky to be together so much more than we were together."

Then pensively she said, "They don't realize it 'cause they've always had each other, just like we didn't realize that life could be the way it is for them."

When she first became a teacher Flora had set her heart on devoting a minimum of forty years to the profession. After her mother became ill she cut that dream to thirty-five years. But, her mother's illness was to become severe enough to force her to miss that goal by three years.

At this time she and a sister, Mrs. Lana Davis, Indianapolis, were the only survivors of the Andrew

Jackson Knight family. The house in which she and her sisters and brother were born, which was built by her father, a white, two-storied frame, stood on a curve on a road which bore the family name – Knightridge. The eventual development of Lake Monroe brought about the demise of the house and the name of the road at that point. Flora was to see the early steps taken to that end.

"But it has changed so," she said of the old home-place and the surrounding neighborhood.

The widow of John Masters, a farmer, Flora spent her later days tending a few tomato plants, reading the daily newspaper, and fixing her own meals.

"All that takes up a good part of my time," she said.

And of her ninety-four years Flora stated, "You just know you're older than everybody else, but you don't think old."

Of course she could not walk miles and ford creeks as she once did, "But," she gratefully pointed out, "I can see, and I can walk."

# FAITH

From the small, shaded front porch where Pallas and Mae Childers sat, a long, curving, gravel drive inclined downward to Washboard Road and one could look down on other homes, fields and trees. It was a secluded, quiet, thoughtful place.

The view would have been the same from a porch swing that was suspended between giant maples in the fenced-in front yard. The seclusion, too. But since they had built the small porch a couple of years earlier the Childers rarely sat on the swing. Pallas was eighty-four and Mae was eighty, and the porch was nearer, easier to get to, and it was easier to just sit on the porch.

"When I first came here this was covered with hawthorn and honey locust," Pallas gestured toward the sloping pasture in front of us where black cows ruminated. "It was the awfullest looking place, and it took a lot of work to clear this land."

That was more than a half-century earlier, a few years after Pallas had left his Kentucky hills home to work in a limestone quarry at Reed Station, near Oolitic. He worked as a laborer there, and as a water boy. One day he was asked to side on an old Sullivan steam channeler, and sometime after that he was given the opportunity to operate one. The work was not easy, but Pallas had come from a hard-working family of eighteen children, and he was prepared for it.

"I was somewhere around the tenth child in the family, I never did bother to count it up," Pallas remembered without humor. "We all worked. Even the girls went to the fields on that hillside, and we worked our corn by hand. It was my job to keep the mules shod, and we plowed with one mule and a double-shovel plow."

At meal times the family ate from a large table built by Pallas's father. They worked six days, and on the seventh, though Pallas's parents were not church-goers, the only work allowed was the feeding of stock.

"There was no church in those Kentucky hills, but once a month or so we'd have church in the school-house," Pallas said.

Perhaps it was in the schoolhouse, once each month, or maybe the influence came from another source, but Pallas as a boy became interested in the Bible. So influenced was he by it that at age twelve, possibly fourteen, he couldn't be sure, he committed himself to a Christian life.

"I prayed to be saved," he said. "There was no church, except what we had in the schoolhouse every month. My parents were good people and as honest as the day is long, but they didn't have much to do with church or the Bible. But I prayed. And the Spirit convicted me when I was a boy. And I never changed."

By this time Pallas had reached that point in life when he had to sit down or lie down to rest during the day. He restricted himself to doing as little as possible – tending a garden, potatoes in rows fifty feet long,

**Pallas and Mae Childers**
On the Porch

corn in rows ninety feet long, beans, tomatoes and cucumbers, and, by all means, going to church.

"Every time the doors are open, we go," he said.

Mae, who was from near Logan, said she was saved at Donica Church.

"When we felt better we went to church every night, if we could find a place to go," she said.

We met after I had received a note from a relative of theirs who wrote to me of Pallas.

"His genuine love and sincere concern are two of his most endearing qualities," the note read. "His faith in God has sustained him all of his life, and sharing that faith is as natural to him as offering our (child) a peppermint stick from the tin on the counter."

From the secluded, small porch on the quiet hill where we sat, Pallas offered to share these words with my readers:

"I am eighty-four years old and I'll soon be eighty-five, and the years have passed so fast it's been like a dream. We don't have long in this life. And the most important thing in it is to live a holy life every day, and to be saved."

# ON BEING ONE HUNDRED

Pete Sloan said that it was a novelty for him to be one hundred years old, novelty being his word and his alone. He explained what he meant in the following manner.

"I can't go anywhere, I can't do anything, I'm just lying here," he said.

"Oh," he went on, "I do get up a few minutes now and then. I go into the kitchen and eat a little and drink a little. But that's my life."

Sloan lived with the mother of his three great grandsons, Lillian Mumby Chitwood, in Bloomington. He'd been there in her home since the day after Christmas, 1982, when Mrs. Chitwood rescued him from what would have been a dreary solitude in Bicknell.

He was not quite one hundred at this time, but that milestone was not that far off, the next January 25. Not enough days from the day of my visit to make his age, at that time, an issue, considering the years he'd piled up toward that credit.

An observer couldn't help but wonder how many old friends remain to a centenarian like that, or – for that matter – how many enemies. In Sloan's case he'd probably outlived them all, except the generous Chitwoods.

"You see them go one by one and pretty soon you're all that's left," a senior lady speaking of friends who were no longer once told me.

She's gone now, too. So is Sloan, of course. But I wonder if there might be someone who may remember him; for years he worked at the Roy Sims Poultry, in Bloomington. That was his line of work: poultryman.

Perhaps I should have checked to see how many well-wishers went over to shake his hand on the 25th, to congratulate him on reaching the century mark. The Chitwoods, to be sure, were there. And there may have been a few cards from readers. Maybe, too, a few packages of Mail Pouch. At ninety-nine and holding at the brink of the Big C a man ought to have one vice, no? Chewing was Sloan's.

"Ninety years," he informed me during a visit to his bedroom. "I've been chewing tobacco ever since I was ten years old."

January 25 was still too distant for Sloan to even hazard a guess about plans for that day. I remember a man on the verge of one hundred who told me that at his age he refused to look past the present. Not even to the next hour, he said.

"Right now I just plan to try to make it till then, and to be here with my people and be good to them," Sloan said of reaching his birthday. "That's my life, too, being good to them."

Sloan, who was difficult to understand because of what might have been a palsied larynx, was silent for a few moments.

"If I feel young enough," he began after the pause, "I'll go outside. I'll get up and go outside. If I can't get up I'll just have to lie here in bed.

"I'm not going to run around," the words had suddenly burst from him. "You can be sure of that. But," he continued wistfully, "I would dance – if I'm able. I did a lot of dancing when I was young."

Although he required attention and assistance, while Mrs. Chitwood was at her job at RCA, Sloan cared for himself. He was often aided by Mrs. Chitwood's three sons who visited the home regularly, and to whom he was grateful.

Looking back on the years to a beginning in Pike County, to coal mining days near Winslow, a job in a poultry house in Oakland City, to poultry houses in Illinois where he was also employed, and some years in Vincennes and other places, Sloan opined that life generally had been good. And he also concluded that given the opportunity he might have been persuaded to do it all over again.

"Those younger years especially," he said with moving honesty, "when I wasn't so old. After you get too old it might not be a pleasure anymore. But my younger days – that is what I'd like to do over again.

"To tell you the truth," he confided with a smile, "I was always pretty handy with the girls then. I always had two or three on the string."

He seemed to enjoy that recollection for a few moments, remaining the while silent, thoughtful. When he spoke again there was a smile on his face and his pale eyes sparkled briefly.

"If I had it to do all over again," his chin bounced up and down, "I'd just kind of take them one at a time."

Until Florence appeared, of course. That's the girl he kept company with for a long time.

"She was my choice over all of the girls," he said. "And when she agreed to have me I married her."

There were no more girls in Sloan's life after that, no more string. And it went on like that for seventy-one years, until November 1982, when Florence passed away at Bicknell.

"She was my life," Sloan said.

Long before he met Florence, however, there was someone else in Sloan's life: the great commoner William Jennings Bryan, a love revealed by a question about Sloan's politics.

"I'm not Democrat and not Republican," he began. "But –" and Sloan was off on the subject of Bryan and his free-silver plank at the Democratic National Convention in Chicago in 1896 – when Sloan was but twelve – and Bryan's electrifying oration in debate there.

"You shall not press down upon the brow of labor this crown of thorns. You shall not crucify mankind upon a cross of gold," Sloan remembered a few of the words that thrilled Bryan's listeners.

Sloan had forgotten the words that preceded those (Having behind us the producing masses of this nation and the world, etc.), but he had not forgotten Bryan. He also remembered that Bryan ran in enough elections (three: twice against William McKinley and once against William Howard Taft) to give a reverent Sloan an opportunity to vote (and remain proud of it) for the three-time loser. When he remembered his attraction to Bryan at age twelve, Sloan noted that, "I had more sense at twelve than I have now."

He had no advice for those who may wish to live to be one hundred.

"No rule," he said. "I lived a good life. Nothing more. And I was good until I was ninety-four. Then one day I went out to care for the dog – the year of the blizzard – and I fell and hit my head. The last six years it's been off and on – I have good days and bad days."

And that, perhaps, was the novelty of which he spoke.

# BERTHA SCHEIBE

It was no time to play Miss Prissy. There were chores to do; splitting firewood, working in the fields, milking, gardening, canning and the regular daily tasks required of a farmer's daughter.

"But," Bertha Scheibe hurried to point out, "It was a nice time to grow up, and I feel that a lot of kids today miss so much because they are not being raised in the country."

Country it was. Eighty acres near Leipsic, where William E. and Cora Wright Hunt settled, labored and reared their two children, Bertha and Frank.

She continued: "We were so busy we didn't have time to go gallivanting around. There were just the two of us to help, and I helped do whatever there was to be done. I did it all. I would even take a team to the field to disk.

"It was an education, and I'm glad I didn't miss it," she said.

There was more education; common school at Leipsic and high school at Orleans, five miles west.

"I drove that distance in a horse and buggy," her face had the tiniest hint of flush as the memory unfolded.

"I had a nice buggy with side springs and a nice driving horse we had named Black Beauty."

When her father needed an extra horse in the fields she drove the family's Model-T Ford to school.

"I had learned to drive when I was just a kid. I was probably thirteen or fourteen, and I used to drive Dr. (G.G.) Colglazier's wife, Madge, around before she learned to drive a car. You didn't need a license to drive one then," she said.

One day, after she'd accepted an invitation to ride to school with a friend, Kathleen Carr, she experienced her only traffic mishap of those early years.

"Kathleen had a steel-tired buggy and a high-stepping horse. On the way to school he kicked the dashboard off the buggy. I was frightened and jumped out just as he lunged and broke loose from the buggy and ran off," she recalled.

She walked to a nearby house unaware that she'd been injured. There she telephoned her father who arrived in due time in her buggy pulled by Black Beauty, and she and Kathleen continued on to school. The next day, however, she was in misery with a sprained ankle she had sustained in the accident and it was two weeks before she could return to classes.

The memories, as she uttered them, gave new warmth and a sense of enchantment to the attractive living room of the Scheibe home in Mitchell. She had lived in that town since her marriage in 1920 to John L. Scheibe.

They had met through friends. He was one of three Mitchell brothers who had served in France at the same time during World War I. The other two were Payot and Fred Scheibe.

John L. – he was John L. to everyone, including his wife – had returned from France to his job as mail carrier at Mitchell and they were married soon after her graduation from Orleans High School. The marriage would last until John L.'s death, more than sixty-one years later on March 31, 1982.

He left behind some golden unforgettables. He carried mail in Mitchell for almost thirty-eight years and then transferred to a rural route which he went on to serve four years. When he wasn't working or assisting his wife in the care of her elderly parents and his elderly parents, John L. was fishing with buddies, Wendell Holmes, Jess Slater, Hugh-Bill Purheiser and Don McNeely. He gave the East Fork of White River and other area fishing holes his very best shot. He had been a member of the First Baptist Church for sixty-six years, and at the time of his passing he had been retired twenty-five years.

Except for the last ten years of his life, when sickness kept him from it, he enjoyed life to the hilt, his widow said.

In addition to Mrs. Scheibe, John L. left a daughter, Mrs. Otis (Betty) Burton, nine grandchildren and numerous great grandchildren. Another grandchild, John Otis Burton, died instantly in an auto accident at age twenty-seven.

Before it fell victim to fire about twenty years prior to my call at her home, Mrs. Scheibe was employed seven years in the Mitchell High School cafeteria. She didn't need the job, but it served to keep her active and involved, as she had been all of her life.

"You have to keep yourself active and involved or you're going to sink," this white-haired, poised woman had said.

In earlier days there was the Great Depression and the unemployed who needed help. Mrs. Scheibe was among a number of responsible citizens who formed a community welfare organization to feed and clothe those victims.

"So many had to have help," she remembered. "And there were some who were willing to do anything to get it. There were an awful lot of people who got help."

She was involved with Tri-Kappa, the American Legion Auxiliary, and her church, the First Baptist, of which she had been a member sixty-two years.

In later years it was the family of grandchildren and great grandchildren who created a new activity, a new interest for her.

"You take all these grandchildren and great grandchildren," she said in calm awe, "and they'll keep you active and involved.

"They're in and out of here all the time, and just being with them keeps me occupied. Just loving them and them loving me seems to keep me feeling good. It helps me keep from feeling my age," she said. Mrs. Scheibe was eighty-two.

When she was not immersed in something else she gave some time to sewing, and to the musical instruments she learned to play as a child; piano and organ as taught to her by Bertie Hordman Oyler who lived near the Liberty Church between Leipsic and Orleans.

"I used to walk a mile to take lessons at her house," Mrs. Scheibe remembered. "They cost fifty cents an hour."

She had enjoyed exceptional health; never sick, never hospitalized. And although some of the grandkids gave her a sweatshirt monogrammed down one side with the word "Mamaw," for her birthday, she had decided that this was no time to play games. And she put her desire to remain in good health in a few amusing words.

"I don't think I'll try jogging," she said with a smile.

# TOMMY AND THE MOUSE

When hot summer nights came to an end that year, Tommy began to sleep better. Trouble was he could not stay asleep. He said he began hearing noises that would wake him. It went on night after night. He'd go to sleep, then the strange noise in his bedroom would disrupt his sleep.

He had been sleeping fitfully all summer because of the rackety exhaust fan he had kept in the bedroom window. Trouble was, the noise that so disturbed his sleep now, the noise that was turning him into a bundle of frazzled nerves, was quite different from that.

"It sounded like a mouse walking across my bedroom floor," he told me and a half dozen or so other acquaintances one night.

We had staged an ad hoc birthday party for Tommy and among the gifts he received was a broken guitar pick wrapped in a piece of toilet tissue, which I had presented to him. Before he started telling us about the noise in his bedroom he'd been using the pick to strum his guitar while singing songs he'd composed.

Slim and light-haired, Tommy, as he sat there speaking to us, wore a struggling waxen beard and a big grin. A guy who should have been suffering from lack of sleep, as he claimed, should not have been grinning like that. But we overlooked that and continued listening to his lamentations.

He said that a mouse nightly walking across his bedroom floor had not only unnerved him and kept him awake, it also had driven him to devise a plan to capture the heavy-footed rodent.

"I bought a mouse trap," he told us, "and I baited it with cheese. I needed to catch that thing so that I could sleep."

And sleep he did. Just setting the trap must have had a tranquilizing effect on Tommy for he slept that entire night, he said.

"But," he added with a show of exasperation, "the next morning the cheese was gone and there was no mouse in the trap. And it was still set."

He had our attention now.

"That mouse," he looked around at each of us as he spoke, "had eaten the cheese and got clean away."

Had he properly set the trap?

He was certain he had.

The mystery deepened.

He reset the trap the next night.

"I piled on the cheese," he said, and for emphasis he began going through the motions of scooping air with one cupped hand and made dumping motions with it into the other hand.

"But," his countenance had taken on a perplexed look, "the next morning the cheese was gone and the trap was still unsprung," he said.

"This," he went on to give us his thoughts of that moment, "has got to be a pretty smart mouse, I said to myself."

He paused to rub his chin whiskers between a

thumb  and index finger, as he must have done that morning.

Then he said again, "This has got to be a pretty smart mouse to be able to remove the cheese from a trap without springing it."

We thought so, too, by this time. Either that was a pretty smart mouse or Tommy's mouse trapping abilities left something to be desired. Before we could suggest anything like that to him his next words gave us pause to reconsider.

"The next night I tied the cheese to the little thing that holds the bait," he salivated at the mere thought of what must have been a brainstorm for him. "I knew that if that little mouse had to struggle for his dinner he'd trip the trap."

For our benefit he chortled gleefully as he must have chortled that night. Then shifting the now long silent guitar from one knee to the other, he said, "Then I went to bed. And I slept good."

Next morning Tommy was again greeted by an empty trap. He took a second look. Indeed, the cheese was gone. The string he'd used to tie it on the trap was still there. Apparently the clever mouse had no use for it. So was the unsprung trap also there.

Flash!

A light bulb suddenly came on in Tommy's brain.

"I knew right then that I had bought a faulty trap," he said. "And I couldn't understand why it hadn't occurred to me before then."

After hearing that, the rest of us also couldn't figure out why that hadn't also occurred to us; it was getting to be a long story. But, it was Tommy's birthday.

With no little amount of chagrin at his failure to test the mouse trap before he had carried it out of the hardware store where he had purchased it, Tommy, that morning in his bedroom, belatedly attempted to test it.

Shifting the guitar pick I had given him for his birthday from his right hand to his left, he demonstrated for us how he had stuck the forefinger of his right hand into the still set trap.

"POW!!!" he suddenly exclaimed.

And jumping straight up from his chair while gripping the guitar by the neck with his left hand as he held it straight out from his body, he wildly shook his right hand in front of him and made pained sounds, as though he'd just got that finger caught in the trap again.

It was an unexpected demonstration of events and the sudden outburst and motion caused the rest of us to very nearly flip backwards in our chairs with surprise.

Tommy paid no attention.

"I was going to get that mouse if it killed me," he roared for the benefit of his listeners as he plopped down in his chair again.

"So I baited the trap again that night. I tied the bait to the little thing you put the bait on again, and I spread newspapers all around and over the trap so that he would have to dig for that cheese.

"Then," he said, instilling further interest in his listeners, "I loaded my B-B gun and got out my flashlight."

Tommy's audience was incredulous. A B-B gun. He was no kid that he should own a B-B gun. Our reaction did not faze him.

"I got myself propped up in bed then," he resumed, "and I switched off the light. I had made up my mind to sit there all night, if necessary. I was determined to shoot me a mouse."

So he waited in the darkness. And he waited, and waited, and waited, he said.

"Then," he had suddenly dropped his voice to just above a whisper, "I heard these footsteps on the newspaper around the mousetrap on the floor. Clump! Clump! Clump! Clump!"

He attempted to imitate the sounds he thought he heard a mouse making as it strode in the darkness of his bedroom toward the baited trap. Wide-eyed glances circled the table. Clump! Clump! Clump! Clump! This had to be the mouse of mice.

"I wanted to flash the flashlight on him right then, but I forced myself to wait," Tommy said, still speaking in that hushed tone.

"No, I said to myself. Wait and see how he's getting the bait off the thing on a mouse trap you put cheese on without springing the trap.

"Then SHOOT him!"

He'd done it to us again. He'd shouted the word SHOOT so loudly he'd just about scared the pants off us.

Resettling ourselves in our chairs we heard Tommy recount how he had waited until he was sure the mouse was eating the cheese off the little bait thing on the trap, and how he took a firm grip on the B-B gun with one hand and switched on the flashlight with the other.

He hesitated.

We waited with baited breath.

"It wasn't even a mouse," he suddenly exclaimed, trying with all his might to re-register the look of astonishment that must surely have spread over his face that night while he held the unseen B-B gun pointing at us in what appeared to be a firing position.

"It was a GREAT, BIG cockroach!!!"

His voice rang out like the peal of a great, big bell. "He was just standing there," Tommy sounded as though he were about to weep, "eating the cheese right off that trap."

Tommy shook his head in perplexity as he certainly must have shaken it that night in his bedroom.

"I never knew that cockroaches ate cheese," he said. "But that one did. He just stood right there and ate every bit of it that I had tied to that little bait thing on the trap.

"Then," Tommy shook his head,"he just turned and walked away.

"CLUMP! CLUMP! CLUMP! CLUMP!"

As he spoke he had set his guitar aside and made crawling motions with his forearms on the table between us.

# INDEX OF NAMES & PLACES

*\*Verse adapted from "Who Has Seen The Wind" by Christina Georgina Rossetti, 1830-1894*

## THE DANCE
Ruth Wrobeleska
Frank Wrobeleska

## THE OLD DEPOT
Owensburg, Greene County
Cleve Smith
Mary Smith
Bob Hudson
The Moss place on Indian
  Creek
Rhelda Horn
Janice Baker
Charlie Miller
Tom Waggoner
Moses Cook
Don Foust
Patsy Foust
Anna Strosnider
Matt Roberts
Uncle Caswell (Cas) Wilson
Curtis Smith

## CLEO
Cleo Kelly Willoughby
Harry Kelley
Nashville
Belmont
Gene Willoughby
Green Valley
Benjamin Roten Kelley
Bill Percifield
Ralph Burkholder
Pleasant Valley
Mabel Burkholder
North Salem
Brown School on Salt
  Creek
Rex Thompson, Jr.
Mary Jane Kelley
Eudora Kelley

## LADY WONDER
Frank Edwards
Lady Wonder
Ronnie Franklin Weitkamp
Crane Village
Crane Naval Ammunition
  Depot
Scotland, In.
Mrs. Edwards
Petersburg, Va.
Washington, D.C.
John Medina
Jim Gentry
Willard Neyhaus

## "MY BRIDGE"
Williams Covered Bridge
  (Monroe County)
Monroe County
Happy Williams
Ellettsville
Ruby McNeely Williams
Wayne W. Williams
M.C. McNeely
Modesto Post Office
Mayor John H. Hooker, Jr.
Ray Cavanaugh
Clyde Lingle Gilbert

## NICKEL BACK
Bedford
Dale Marley
Jesse Marley
Jim Marley
Bill Marley
Clarence Mosier
Trinity Springs
Lowell Smith
Otho Smith
Raymond Stultz
Kathryn Parker Marley
Bob Mellen, Esq.

## MATTIE FAUBION
Mattie Faubion
Heltonville
Jep Newkirk
Scott Clampitt
Elmer Ramsey
George Ross
Fanny Thomas

## THE PROUD FIREMAN
Bloomington
Harry McNeeley
Hollis "Ditty" Van Dyke
Noble Henderson
Bernard Glover
Cotton Brandt
Loba "Jack" Bruner
Bert Hazel
Leon Dillman
Horace Robertson
Rollie Crum
Ray Collier
Paul Lentz
Carl Hawkins
Millard Axsom
Fred Koontz
Roger Coan
John Thrasher
Silas Crum
Willis Lawhead
Clarence Brewer
Arthur Retzlaff
Jewitt Wampler
Monroe County
Solsberry
Tom Lemon
Mary Alice Dunlap
Robert Glover
Richard Glover
Gordon Glover
Philip "Bud" Glover
C. Earl East
Maude Williams Glover

## THE MUSICIANS
Ellen Wright (Aunt Ellie)
Tunnelton
Aunt Ellen Wilcox
John R. Smith
Terri McCart
Mabel Smith
Paula Dorsett
Lawrenceport
Susan Weaver
Bono
Medora
Vallonia

## THE OLD MAN
The old man

## DOVIE
Dovie Dillard
French Lick
Tom Taggart, Sr.
Al Smith
Herbert Hoover
Tom Mix
Gov. Paul V. McNutt
Irene Castle
Franklin D. Roosevelt
Thomas Meehan
Douglas Fairbanks
Mary Pickford
Rolla Dillard
Paoli
Orleans

## LOST CEMETERY
Lake Monroe
Heltonville
Dwight Jones
Leston Jones
Daniel Fox Cemetery
Hughes Cemetery
Macy Malott Cemetery
Daniel Fox Cemetery
Russell Mitchell Cemetery

Blackwell Cemetery
Clear Creek Cemetery
   at Harrodsburg
Shields Cemetery
Allens Creek Cemetery
Cutright Cemetery

THE CAMP
   Homer Spriggs
   Mutt
   Icis Spriggs
   Benton Township
   Brummetts Creek Road
     near Brown County Line
   Monroe County
   Noble Spriggs
   Mable Spriggs
   George Spriggs
   Ella Carpenter, Tucson, AR.

THE DREAM
   Raymond Ashby
   Sarah Ashby
   White River
   Worthington
   Indianapolis
   The Whale House

THE LETTER
   The Prisoner

OLD JOSH
   Josh
   Biddy
   Biddy's father
   Biddy's mother

SAVORY INDIANA
   Earl Whaley
   Irene Whaley
   Allie Sparks
   Ethel Sparks
   Elwren

Blair Hollow
Blair School
Stanford
Lucy Rowe
Charlie Hudson
John Ellen
Tanny Walker
Andy Walker
Bloomington
Hendricksville
Blutcher Poole
Uncle Bob Fowler
John Ballinger
McHaley and Isom
Bill Yoho
Orville Barnes
Edgar Helms
Ezra Dyer

FLORA KNIGHT MASTERS
   Flora
   Friendship
   Bloomington
   Andrew Jackson Knight
   Amanda Terrell Knight
   Florence Chambers
   Lana Davis
   John Masters

FAITH
   Pallas Childers
   Mae Childers
   Reed Station
   Oolitic
   Kentucky
   Logan
   Donica Church

ON BEING ONE HUNDRED
   Pete Sloan
   Lillian Mumby Chitwood
   Bicknell

Bloomington
Pike County
Winslow
Oakland City
Vincennes
Florence Sloan
William Jennings Bryan

BERTHA SCHEIBE
Bertha Scheibe
Leipsic
William E. Hunt
Cora Wright Hunt
Frank Hunt
Orleans
Dr. G. G. Colglazier
Madge Colglazier
Kathleen Carr
Mitchell
John L. Scheibe
Payot Scheibe
Fred Scheibe
Wendell Holmes
Jess Slater
Hugh-Bill Purheiser
Don McNeely
Mrs. Otis (Betty) Burton
John Otis Burton
Bertie Hordman Oyler

TOMMY AND THE MOUSE
Tommy

# THE WIND CHIME TALES

To order extra copies of Larry Incollingo's books
please fill out the coupon below and mail to:

### REUNION BOOKS
3949 Old SR 446
Bloomington, IN 47401-9747

*For multiple order special discounts (three or more books)
call 812-336-8403.*

Please send me:

_____ copies of *The Wind Chime Tales* @ $10.50 each

_____ copies of *The Tin Can Man* @ $10.50 each

_____ copies of *ECHOES of Journeys Past* @$10.50 each

_____ copies of *Ol' Sam Payton* @ $9.50 each

_____ copies of *Precious Rascal* @ $9.50 each

_____ copies of *G'bye My Honey* @ $9.50 each

_____ copies of *Laughing All The Way* @ $9.50 each

      *Add 5% Sales Tax, Plus $2 M&H (up to three books)*

_____

NAME

_____

ADDRESS              CITY            STATE

_____

ZIP         TELEPHONE

## SEND A GIFT COPY TO A FRIEND

Autograph to:

_____